I0556819

WUNDERLING

ERIC SUDDOTH

RISING SMOKE PUBLISHING

Rising Smoke Publishing
ISBN 978-1-949869-23-1

wun·der·ling *noun*
: a person attributed to supernatural powers or a miraculous ability

CHAPTER 1

"Grandma, I'm sorry, but I just couldn't wake up in time," Lao lied over the phone as he scurried around his bedroom, rummaging through his dirty clothes on the green shaggy carpet floor. He was looking for the high school swimming hoodie he'd gotten two years ago as a freshman.

"Next Sunday, Laonardo," his grandmother said warmly. "Next Sunday you'll come to church with me, and then I'll treat you to lunch."

"Uh huh," he answered passively, not giving his mother's mom the attention she deserved, as he had other things on his mind. His eyes lit up as he saw a gray sleeve sticking out from under his bed. He pulled on the cotton fabric as his grandmother continued to ramble. He smiled as his school's logo and mascot shone like neon lights, even though the dismal acrylic crimson paint was flaking off. The Red Devils of Sardis High School looked more like a caricature than a fierce school to be reckoned with.

"I gotta go, Grandma," Lao rushed as he heard her gush and plead for him to call her this week.

"And I'll see you Sunday at church," she said as he ended the call.

He lifted the sweatshirt to his face and sniffed. The smell wasn't pleasing, but a few sprays of cologne would mask the musky smell of teenager hormones. He left his room, putting on his sweatshirt as he walked down the dimly lit hallway that segued into the living room and kitchen.

His mother was standing at the kitchen counter eating a scoop of peanut butter while reading the newspaper. She had recently gotten home from her shift as a nurse at Sardis Regional Hospital and was catching up on the daily news before pouring a glass of wine and taking a bubble bath.

1

"I see you didn't make any supper," she said as Lao stopped dead in his tracks, wincing at the forgotten note on the refrigerator door.

"I'm sor--" he started, but his mother didn't care for his regret.

"Does it do me any good to leave a note for you? All you had to do was stick the casserole — the casserole *I* made — in the oven for 45 minutes. But no, you couldn't even leave your bedroom to fix us a nice meal for a change," she lectured, pulling herself away from the obituaries to look at him.

He looked at her with contempt. This wasn't the first time he had forgotten, and he knew it probably wouldn't be the last.

"You have nothing to say?" she asked, bitter from years of working as a single mom with no recognition of a job well done.

"I'm going out." He thought about apologizing, but she'd cut him off a minute earlier, and he knew nothing he could say would help. At least, that was what he remembered hearing his dad say the last time he'd heard his voice when he was eight.

He waited for her to say something, but she returned her gaze to the newspaper and the half-eaten spoon of creamy peanut butter. They didn't have the best relationship, and there was nothing he could do to fix it. His name, Laonardo, was supposed to be Leonardo, but his own father couldn't spell it right when the nurse asked for the newborn's name. Every time Lao had to correct someone who called him Leonardo by accident, it reminded him that if his mother truly loved him, she would have easily fixed the spelling error. But she never did. That was proof to Lao that from the very beginning, his mother saw him as only a mistake.

He turned and left their apartment, rushing down the three flights of stairs. He opened the door and felt the coolness of autumn hit his face and hands. He lifted his hood over his ears and walked through the parking lot. He looked ahead and saw the golden sun sitting in the distance, causing the sky to explode with streaks of reds and oranges, colors that matched the leaves that had already fallen to their fate in the changing seasons.

He walked down the sidewalk, noticing fully decorated homes with haystacks and corn stalks on their front porches with families of carved jack-o'-lanterns meticulously placed like stockings at Christmastime.

He used to enjoy Halloween as a kid, but now it was just a day. Just another day that meant nothing to him anymore.

Where are you at? Thya, his girlfriend, texted.

I'm on my way, he replied as he smiled.

Okay. I got all the stuff. I'm excited.

Scared? he asked, as he enjoyed playing with her.

Never. You?

Nope. He recalled all the scary movies they had watched over the last three weeks, and none of them had seemed believable.

Well, get here quick. The sun will be down soon and then we will start.

What? Do you expect the ghosts to be gone soon?

You think you're funny, don't you?

He read the last message from Thya and grinned a little more. He did think he was funny. He expected nothing to happen tonight. It was just going to be a fun night to kick back, drink a little, and hang out with friends in a local cemetery.

The séance might just be a rouse, but he didn't care. He wasn't interested in conjuring the dead or speaking to spirits from long ago. He just wanted to be around his friends tonight.

Candles and all, on O'Hallow's Eve.

3

CHAPTER 2

The red-golden sky quickly dissolved into a purple haze as the sun disappeared beyond the horizon. The sidewalks of the upper-class neighborhood of Sardis were lit with flickering old -fashioned gas-fueled streetlamps. The flames danced behind the glass enclosures like flamenco dancers with their ruffled skirts that spun and swayed to the rhythm of the music.

Lao lifted his eyes from the bricked sidewalk and glanced over at the three-story home with its plantation styled front porch. The neatly decorated white banisters with white wicker furniture, and the floral pillows beckoned neighbors to stop by for a visit and a glass of lemonade. He rolled his eyes at the opulence but smiled at the newly lit lopsided pumpkin carvings. He stared at the disfigured gourd that looked to be sliced with childish hands.

He remembered being a kid carving a similar pumpkin while his mother sautéed the seeds in the kitchen with a mixture of seasonings that would awaken even the dullest of taste buds. He used to love Halloween with the childish intrigue of dressing up and pretending to be someone else.

Now he realized life wasn't like that. No matter how much you dress up and pretend to be someone else, you can never outrun your family tree. If you were born as a descendent of a white-trash gene pool, you were going to grow up with the same nametag.

Kryptonite was nothing compared to a poor reputation in small-town gossip. Superman couldn't outrun the snickers of the high school hallways or stop the speeding arrows of the hurtful taunting in the locker room. Costumes couldn't hide the truth.

He shook off the memories of his jaded childhood like they were a cape attached to his shoulder. But just like a cape, the memories were always going to be hauntingly near him. No matter how fast he ran, or how high he jumped, or how swiftly he swam, he could never flee the nagging knot tied around his neck like a noose.

At least a noose would be less painful than years of ridicule.

He closed his eyes, wishing he hadn't trekked down that lonely path in his subconscious. He came to a crosswalk and took a step out onto the road. He felt a sudden gust of wind, causing his shaggy head of blond hair to slip away from the hoodie, drooping over his jade-green eyes. He felt the coolness of the wind, carrying him like a fallen leaf to a state of utopia. He took another step, his foot dangling inches above the street as a sudden jolt of fear seized his insides. A car horn blared a blood-curdling shrill as he felt an icy hand pulling him back onto the curb.

Lao fell back and watched without any breath in his lungs as the vehicle sped away. He had never known what it felt like to have his breath stolen. He didn't know how to describe it as he stood up and swayed on the curb, watching the taillights of the Mazda CX-3 dart away as the driver gunned his engine, quickly reaching the 45 mile per hour speed limit in four seconds flat. He felt alive for the first time in years.

Some would think a near-death experience would bring a sense of gratitude for survival, but Lao didn't feel that emotion. He liked the grizzly touch of near-death. He liked that feeling of almost losing it all.

He liked it because a second ago he didn't realize he had anything to lose.

It took a split second to wake him to what he was overlooking.

He looked down at his hands that usually trembled and shook secretly in his blue jean pockets, but not anymore. They felt strong. They felt fierce. They felt alive. He could feel the power in his veins.

He was never one to partake in the act of cutting, but he understood the victim's need. The need to feel something, even if it was the piercing of skin from a razor blade to sense the trickle of red life on death-like flesh.

A smile radiated from his lips as he watched the Mazda move off into the distance, vanishing under the indigo sky. He wanted to yell his thanks to the guy almost killing him tonight.

It was like it jolted him awake.

He was done with going through the motions.

He was ready to feel that shock of life more often.

He stepped off the curb and looked both ways. This time, his path was clear. He walked across the empty road and stepped over the cement curb. The sidewalk continued, but he decided to walk down the unclear path through a wooded area. The forest sat on the outskirts of town, forming the boundary line for the city limits of Sardis. He knew he could have walked on the bricked sidewalk to reach his destination, but he felt he needed to live a little tonight.

Tonight was the start of a new way of living.

CHAPTER 3

The sound of the traffic faded into rustling leaves and creaking branches as Lao walked further into the darkening forest. He looked overhead, the bare treetops whose limbs intertwined, forming a lifeless dome replaced the peaceful indigo sky. Squinting his eyes, he tried to make out the details and the height of the natural roof, but all he could see was a shaded ceiling. He expected to see an occasional blue hue from a break in the forest's weaving canopy, but it was solid, as if a master carpenter bound and connected the limbs for the woodland creatures' protection.

He walked casually, enjoying the sound of mother nature. He closed his eyes and walked down the blinding path, taking in the musings of the dried leaves crunching underneath his black Converse. He smiled as he recalled memories of raking up mounds of fallen leaves behind his apartment building with the neighbor kids and jumping into the piles.

He took another step and heard something different. The cracking of a twig roared over the muffled leaves. He felt the stick under his foot break under his weight. He took another step and heard another high-pitched snap from below. He shuffled his feet along the dirt path, wading through the ankle-deep pool of leaves.

His eyes jolted open as his body froze. The leaves around his feet ceased their movements as well. He listened intently, holding his breath. Then he heard it again.

Snap.

He spun around, thinking he heard the breaking of a tree branch behind him. But he found himself alone. He strained his eyes to see the entrance of the path, but he had been walking for ten minutes. He couldn't see where he'd entered anymore.

Snap.

He darted around, thinking the sound came from in front of him now. He looked ahead for the exit of this path, but he couldn't see the end. He was somewhere in the middle of the forest. At least, he hoped it was the middle.

Snap.

He turned his head around, trying to figure out where the sounds were coming from. He pulled out his phone, but his screen signaled no reception. But that bit of light caused him to feel a little more at ease. He may not be able to call someone, but at least he wasn't in the dark. He hit a button and his phone's flashlight illuminated a dismal haze five feet in front of him. It wasn't much, but it was better than nothing.

Hoo. Hoo. Hoo. A lonely owl sounded from the trees. Lao held his phone ahead of him as he took another step and the rustling leaves once again filled his ears. "It's just a rabbit," he told himself as he walked. "It's only a rabbit."

Hoo. Hoo. Hoo. The owl seemed to question him.

Suddenly, he heard a loud splintering break that was much thicker than the previous twigs snapping.

"That must have been a deer," he affirmed to himself as he walked a little faster, kicking up the leaves with each step.

Once again, his ears perked to a loud break behind him. He inhaled a deep breath and ran. He held the phone up, letting the light shine as much as it could, but the little light wasn't enough as he felt a low-hanging tree branch swipe its bare limb across his cheek.

He screamed out in shock, which quickly turned to a spontaneous round of laughter. He stopped walking as he realized he was letting his fear get the best of him.

"It's just a tree branch," he told himself as he turned around, shining his light back, expecting to see a bush or tree limb reaching into the path. But there wasn't anything there. There was no leafless branch anywhere near the path.

His insides froze as he spun around and ran as fast as he could. He couldn't see what was in front of him. He wasn't even holding his phone up anymore. His arms were swinging back and forth like a track star at the Olympics. He didn't know where he was running. He only knew he needed to outrun whatever was behind him.

He continued to run as if his life depended on it. He didn't want his memory to go any further. He didn't want to remember what else he saw. He just wanted to pretend like it was a figment of his imagination. That he saw a tree limb that slid past his cheek.

But he couldn't believe that. Because there was no tree limb. There was no bush.

But he saw something—a robed shadowed figure slinking behind a tree trunk.

Hoo. Hoo. Hoo.

It was nothing, he told himself as he continued to run. But he knew that was a lie.

He didn't know what was freakier, seeing the back of the creature hide behind the tree or watching the creature grip onto the bark of the rotting tree with long skinny fingers as if it was watching him.

Watching him with fingers that looked like they would feel like leafless tree limbs.

Snap.

CHAPTER 4

He ran. He tried to push away the memory of the skeleton-like fingers clutching onto the tree bark. The fingers that caressed his right cheek like his mother used to when snatching a fallen eyelash from his skin. The lifeless dead hand that was cold to the touch.

He heard no more sounds in the forest. Complete void. He had been on local swim teams since his father had flung him into Mr. Wormwood's crummy little pond when he was five years old. It was sink or swim time. The memory of looking up through the water's ripple-free surface still haunted his dreams. The smug smile of his father, who was talking carelessly to Mr. Wormwood as Lao's little mouth was screaming, allowing water to fill him. He remembered watching as the air bubbles escaped his mouth, rising to the surface. He had followed the little droplets of air like breadcrumbs, but there wasn't a witch on the dock. Just his father and ol' Mr. Wormwood waiting with a fresh beer in hand.

He wasn't the best on Sardis High School's swim team. That titled belonged to Reid Richland. He always won the freestyle races as Lao was lucky to even medal, even in practices with six swimmers. He wasn't the fastest, but he had stamina.

He continued to run. His speed was parting the leaves, forming a trail like a farmer plowing his field, digging into the solid earth. He glanced ahead but couldn't see a break in the forest. He had walked through this forest a few times before, but it never seemed like this.

But he had never seen what he just saw either.

He reached deep and continued to sprint. Suddenly, his ears perked up. *What was that?* he asked himself as he continued to run while the wind picked up, causing his hoodie to slide off his head.

He heard it again. It was a loud creaking and grinding echo that magnified from his fear. He didn't look behind him. He continued to run. When he heard it again with a powerful gust of wind, it almost veered him off his course, as if hurricane force gales were bearing down on him. He felt pummeled by the ferocious gusts, but he didn't let up his pace.

Crash!

He jumped back as he let out a gasp. He couldn't audibly scream. He stood in shock. His eyes glistened, either through tears or sweat, but he couldn't ignore how close he came to death. He stopped for what seemed like an hour, but was really just two seconds as he stared at the branch thicker than his waist. He wondered if he'd been just two steps further if that fallen log would have smashed onto him. If he was just a split second faster, would he be dead right now?

The wind stopped, concluding as fast as it was birthed. As if it was meant just for him.

He hurdled over the log and ran.

The noises he had heard a few minutes ago were silent. The owls had vanished. The snapping branches had strengthened. The creaking, swaying limbs had frozen in place. It was like nothing had happened.

He spotted the exit and, through the parting of the trees, vehicle taillights cruising down the road. He smiled, feeling the relief of this episode ending. With every stride, he felt a little more reassurance. His love of autumn was returning as he watched the light from his phone hit the ground and saw the colorful assortment of leaves around his feet.

Moron, he thought as he looked up and saw he was just twenty feet away. He wondered if he really saw what he thought he did or if his imagination was getting the better of him. He quickly decided he had spent too many evenings with his girlfriend and friends lately, trying to conjure spirits. Spirits he didn't believe in. *Ghosts are not real,* he said to himself.

Hoo. Hoo. Hoo. The owl once again revealed himself to his guest.

Lao took two more long strides and felt the freedom of leaving the forest. He bent over, allowing his body to rest. He inhaled deeply and wiped a few beads of sweat off his forehead.

He stood up and watched a vehicle slowly pass by.

Hoo. Hoo. Hoo. The owl seemed to bid him a farewell.

He turned back to look into the forest, but he couldn't see into the blackness because of the canopy of woven limbs. He stared into the wooded area, feeling foolish for allowing his mind to ambush his logic. He stood safely a few feet from the paved sidewalk and a few feet from the leafy path. He was at a crossroads, per se, between moving on or going back.

Someone was beckoning him to come back into the woods. He couldn't understand it. While he was in there, he wanted nothing more than to leave, but now he had left, he wanted to return and overcome his irrational fear.

He stepped back into the forest, allowing his eyes to adjust to the darkness. He stood in the entryway and looked around, shuffling his feet, tossing the leaves from side to side. He felt safe.

When his phone vibrated, he looked down and saw it was his girlfriend checking on him. He quickly texted back saying he would be there soon. He put up his phone as he heard a muffler coming up the road. He was about to turn as the lights from the pickup truck shone behind him, lighting up the darkness for a split second.

His eyes went wide; his legs went limp. He fell back, colliding with the hard, cold ground. He scrambled, clawing his hands into the dirt, embedding his nails with woodsy soil. His insides churned as he turned over, crawling onto his hands and knees to flee what he saw once again.

It wasn't his imagination.

He stood up and started running on the sidewalk. He pulled out his phone and dialed his girlfriend, whose phone went straight to voicemail.

He continued to run as cars shone their bright lights on his back as they passed. He loved the knowledge of people seeing him, but he loathed the feeling of the light hitting his back. Every time a car passed him from behind, he flashed back to standing at the woods' entrance as the pickup truck's light shone around him.

He tried to shake off the vision, but it was embedded in his mind.

The car passed and so did the light.

"It's going to be okay," he declared to himself as his pace slowed. "That was just your imagination. That was just your imagination. That was just your imagination," he repeated to himself for the next minute, trying to convince himself.

He watched as a vehicle started coming toward him. The red sports car's lights shone into the distance, showing proof of what was in its path. The car curved with the road and the light pierced into Lao's eyes, blinding him for a moment.

He stood, allowing his vision to return, but in that brief moment of pause when he couldn't see anything, he remembered everything he saw with perfect clarity.

He wrung his hands, feeling the caked-on dirt. He didn't want to admit what he'd seen, but he couldn't deny it. No self-talk could erase that memory.

It was like what he saw earlier, but much clearer. It was as clear as under a full harvest moon. His heart plummeted as he succumbed to the truth. He didn't want to acknowledge he saw it stand, raising its skeleton-like hands to the sky. He didn't want to tell himself it looked just like what he'd seen earlier.

He didn't want to believe it, but he couldn't deny it either.

Lao only saw the creature for a second, but he got an understanding of what he was doing. It was as if the robed figure was controlling the force of nature.

It was as if it was trying to control him.

CHAPTER 5

"You're almost there," he told himself as he walked down a deserted alley behind a row of shotgun style homes built in the 1950s after the troops returned home from war and the baby boomers surged into the hospital delivery rooms. A couple of homes had a back porch light on, but the glow shining from the singular bulb wasn't enough to illuminate the gravel he was walking on.

He stuck his hands into his sweatshirt front pockets and warmed them for a little while. He didn't know if it was the weather or the morbid chill he was trying to shake off. He didn't want to think back to his journey in the woods, but it seemed like every new thought circled back to that mysterious figure.

His stride shortened as he heard a faint whistle in the distance. It wasn't the wind causing the high-pitched shrill. It was a mouth. His ears perked as he tried to use his keen hearing like a compass to find the direction it was coming from. He spun in a slow circle, but it seemed like whatever direction he stared, the sound was always coming from behind.

He stopped in the middle of the gravel alley and closed his eyes. The whistling got louder as his sense of hearing magnified the volume, while his other senses faded. He identified the whistler's direction. He kept his eyes closed and walked in its direction. He couldn't tell which direction he was walking, but he knew he was still on the gravel path based upon the shuffling of rocks beneath his feet.

The fear was subsiding. Even though he was walking blindly, he wasn't afraid of the unknown whistler. With every step he took, the sound of the melody became stronger and heavier. He wanted to whistle too, but that was a feat he had never mastered, no matter how many times he had tried to pucker his lips and blow.

He walked with a renewed strength in his legs and a speed in his step. He didn't know what it was, but he was feeling drawn to this sound. It was as if while he remained focused on that sound, his attention couldn't dart or ebb back to what he didn't want to think about. He felt his phone vibrate in his pocket, but he didn't feel like losing his momentum. He knew it was just Thya wondering where in the world he was. If given a second to think, he would wonder about that same question, but he didn't. He just listened to the continual whistle.

He felt like he was on top of the whistler, like it was within inches of his face. He took another couple of steps forward, but it seemed like it had barely faded. He stopped and listened with all his might.

He took a step back, and it slightly got louder. He took another step and once again it got just a little louder. He continued back until he found the sweet spot of the highest decibel. He stood there and listened. He knew without a doubt he had found the place with the music man or woman, probably sitting on their back porch, enjoying one of the last autumn nights before the nighttime air would start to be unbearably cold.

He opened his eyes, expecting to see what he had envisioned.

He was wrong.

He turned around to see the last house in the row was fifty feet behind him. He had stopped in front of a clearing with no human in sight. There was no home. There was no back porch. There was no man or woman sitting under the stars whistling a peaceful tune.

The clouds parted overhead, causing the full moon to shine in all of its splendid glory, reflecting the sun's light down onto the illuminated meadow. He strained his eyes, thinking he would find someone, anyone, lying in the middle of the field. He took a step off the gravel path and planted his right foot on the grassy field. The melody got an eerie feel, but he didn't know if the feeling was based more upon confusion or fear.

He walked further into the clearing as the whistling sounded with perfect clarity. He looked around the grassy field, walking as if at midday with the brightness of the moon's light overhead. His eyes had adjusted, and everything was visible.

Everything.

But even though he could see everything, he couldn't see the one thing he wanted to see.

"Hello?" His voice quivered standing in the middle of the field.

Silence. The whistling stopped immediately in mid-blow.

"I'm sorry to bother you," Lao apologized as he stood perfectly still and looked around in all directions. There wasn't a figure lying anywhere in the grass as far as his eyes could see.

"It was just really beautiful." He thought the compliment would rouse the whistler to acknowledge Lao, but it didn't.

"Well," Lao said as he was about to turn to leave. "You have a good evening."

When he turned to leave, the whistling started again.

Lao froze, quickly turning hoping to find the musician with his playfulness.

The whistling froze as well.

Lao scratched his head as he surveyed the land, but there was nothing to see. He was alone.

As soon as he thought about that menacing notion, his mind quickly sprinted back to the figure in the woods.

Maybe I'm not alone, he thought.

He imagined his heart pounding like percussion drums in the high school band. He turned to flee the open field that still felt secluded.

The whistling started once again.

But this time, instead of whistling a tune. It whistled sharp terse notes over and over.

It was matching Lao's steps, as if commanding him to march away. As if warning him to not stop and turn around. As if the hidden figure was telling him to leave.

Now.

CHAPTER 6

Lao started running down the gravel road, leaving the darkened homes and grassy field in his tracks as he clutched his ears. He could still hear the whistler give off short, fast gusts of wind with each stride.

He wanted to escape into silence.

He ran at full force, leaving his fear in the background as he hummed. He wanted to tune out the haunting whistling. He hummed under the blackened sky, as if singing a song for the sleeping critters nearby.

The gravel road turned into a dirt path. He looked up and saw the little country church up on the hill that oozed simplicity and charm. He was almost at his destination.

He sprinted up the path, slick from the rain the day before. He started climbing the hill and realized he could see past the meadow and homes. The gravel road looked like a tiny white stream that thinned and vanished under the moonlit sky. He squinted his eyes, but everything blurred into the horizon.

"Finally," he heard Phil say from behind.

Lao turned around, fixating his focus on a new subject – his friends. Suddenly, he felt like the last hour was a strange, unreal dream.

"Did you get lost?" Thya asked as she wrapped her arms around Lao's neck.

He brushed off the question with a grin. "Lost? In this town?"

"She was getting worried about you," Smyrna, the last member of the group said, coming out of the church's shadow.

"You were worried about me?" Lao smiled, leaning in to kiss Thya on her lips, but she missed her cue and turned her head, eyeing Smyrna suspiciously.

"I don't worry," Thya assured firmly to Smyrna, then turned her head, almost bumping into Lao's forehead as their noses touched.

"You don't?" Lao grinned as he leaned in a second time. This time, she leaned in as well.

"Come on." Phil commanded as he left the trio, hiking up the dirt path past the chapel.

"What's wrong with him?" Thya asked, looking over at Smyrna.

"You know, Phil." She shrugged her shoulders and grinned watching her first teenage love walk ahead of them.

Phil walked ahead of the group with his black ensemble of jeans, combat boots, and Marilyn Manson t-shirt that matched his slick gelled midnight black hair and thick eyeliner.

Smyrna, Phil's girlfriend of seven months, wore her short black skirt and fishnet stockings with her gold letter W sweater, reminiscent of Nathaniel Hawthorne's scarlet A. But instead of adulterer, she wore the title of witch proudly.

Thya's and Lao's blue jeans and school sweatshirt attire may not fit with the evening, but Lao didn't think the spirits would care what they were wearing. That was, until an hour ago.

"Are you sure about this?" Lao whispered into her ear as Smyrna skipped ahead to catch up with Phil.

"Come on," Thya bargained tenderly. "This is the last night of these séances for a while."

"I just…" Lao started and then stopped. He didn't know what to say. He didn't want to alarm her. Or look like a fool to the gang. He didn't even want to admit to himself something wasn't right about this.

"What?" Thya asked as she leaned her head onto his shoulder as they walked.

Lao thought back over the last three nights of these séances. Thursday night Phil took the lead and offered his body to the spirits. Friday night Smyrna followed. Nothing seemed to happen, so Lao played along and offered his body up to the spirits. He thought nothing of it until an hour ago, when he'd started seeing things he had never seen before.

He had walked this same path three nights before and he had never experienced the haunting chill of unexplained events as he had tonight.

"Just let Phil do it again tonight," Lao urged softly. "He won't get another chance until next year."

"But I didn't get a turn." She looked up into Lao's eyes, giving him a playful smile as they walked conjoined.

"You're not missing anything.".

"You're not telling me something." Thya stopped and scooted away from Lao's strong shoulder. She looked Lao in the eyes while he tried to skirt away from the interrogation.

"There's nothing to tell," he maintained, grabbing her hand. Thya quickly pulled it back and stepped in front of Lao so their eyes connected.

"What are you hiding?"

Lao blinked. He knew Thya had a gift of knowing when to call someone on their bluff. He had learned that last year when she'd accused her last boyfriend, Carson, of lying to her. Which he had. But it was a stupid lie, nothing really important that should have ended their relationship. But she knew he was lying with just a look, and in a split second, it was over. Lao had used that wedge and slid into potential boyfriend status.

"I...," he started, when she placed a finger on his lips.

"You know if you lie, I will know," she threatened treacherously, with a slight grin.

He nodded his head. "I know."

"What do you know?" she returned inquisitively.

He thought for a second. Whatever answer he gave wouldn't be enough to please her. His mind flashed back to the creature in the woods, the whistling in the meadow, the chill in his stomach. Regardless of what he said, she would either dump him for being a chicken or for lying.

That is unless he told her the truth.

"More than you know." He looked into her eyes. "More than you know."

CHAPTER 7

The quaint, countryside church, with its tall slender steeple and a lightning rod of a cross at the top, looked like a forgotten eyesore under the harvest moon. The clouds ebbed into the sky, causing the light to lessen its friendly glow into a chilling taste of dread and caution. The blanket of cottony grays fully eclipsed the twinkling stars and radiant moon.

Lao cast a long look over at the church, and his heart felt a tug to turn away. The brightly colored stained-glass windows looked worn and dingy, as if they needed to be boarded up to cause any unlikely pilgrim to keep moving to the next sanctuary of grace and mercy. He didn't feel the warmth of goodwill and charity that should exude from the two white front doors. He felt the icy presence of lock and key. He stared up at the steeple realizing the church didn't have the stereotypical bell. He had come to this same location for the last three nights, but he hadn't noticed this detail.

"What are you looking at?" Thya asked, squeezing Lao's hand and tugging him down beside her to sit in a circle around Ambrose Lunderbrooke's tombstone.

He shook off the question and sat on the blanket Smyrna had laid out.

"Shall we begin?" Phil questioned, his tone sounding more like a command.

Smyrna pulled out her candles from her satchel, precisely aligning the various sizes and colors atop the tombstone.

"May this light we ignite bring forth life to us tonight," Smyrna vowed poetically as she struck a match against the granite rock. The flame tore through the darkness, causing it to flee. "Repeat after me," she requested as she looked around the group of misfits. "I light this candle to bring forth the past."

23

The three repeated her line in a ritualistic monotone as a soft glow strengthened on the tall gray candle.

"I light this candle to bring forth the present." She lowered the long match to the shorter crimson tier.

They once again repeated her line.

"I light this candle to bring forth the future." She watched enthusiastically as the ivory candle sparked a white glow.

The three repeated her line once again.

"With these three, we become one," she yelled as she closed her eyes and lifted her hands. "With these three, we become one."

She continued to chant this line as Phil and Thya joined in, lifting their hands and closing their eyes. Lao watched uneasily, the volume of his words fading to a mumble as he watched his surroundings. The three chanters' voices climbed in eager anticipation, with urgency and desire to see their wishes come true. As the spells were being shouted, Lao's hearing faded. It was as if he was being taken far away into another realm.

He looked around at the scenery of the graveyard behind the country church. He looked ahead at the tombstone as he reached out his hand and traced the dates chiseled into the rock, the life and time of Mr. Lunderbrooke.

His ears perked as a strange sound cut through the silence and a cold bead of sweat slid down his forehead to his temple. It felt like the singular droplet of fear froze on his skin. He reached up to his head and felt the sweat was hard to his touch.

He heard the sound again as his stomach lurched in dread. His eyes darted around the circle, seeing the expressions of ecstasy on each of their faces. He opened his mouth and tried to speak, but nothing came forth.

The sound was getting louder. It was coming closer. He could feel it in his core and it hurt. He felt like he was being punched in the sides, but he couldn't move. He couldn't flinch. He couldn't block the jabs.

The haunting melody was returning, and it was coming with a vengeance. The whistler was coming. Lao once again tried to say a word, but he felt his vocal cords snap. He wanted to scream from the pain, but all he could do was look ahead with his hand still clutching his temple.

He was paralyzed, yet sitting upright. His mouth gaped wide as his eyes fluttered like manic bumblebees looking for someone to sting. He had three people in sight, but nothing to sting them with.

His eyes rushed to Phil who was sitting on his left and shedding a few tears from his emotional plea. He watched Phil for what seemed like an hour as he continued to chant and recite the words like gospel. Lao's eyes lifted higher up Phil's arm as the veins in his hands protruded out of his flesh. His hands were locked in a tight grip as his arms trembled and shook with a violent quake.

Lao moved his attention to Smyrna who was sitting across from him on the other side of Ambrose's headstone. She looked to be in a battle trance as her eyelids fluttered like during a seizure. He looked up at her lips and noticed she wasn't saying the same words as Phil. Her lips were dancing chaotically as her tongue flopped in and out of her mouth like a fish trying to find water. He watched, but he couldn't make out what she was saying. All he could hear was the sound of the whistling blaring like a foghorn in his ears. He looked behind her and saw a shadowed figure. It was a shadow that hadn't been there at the start of the night. It wasn't moving, but he didn't feel safe.

He slowly traced Smyrna's outline with his eyes as he looked over to Thya who was sitting to his right. Her lips quivered in uninvited fear as she continued to say the inviting words. He wanted nothing more than to reach over and touch her hand, but he was stuck in this state of

25

purgatory. His watchful eyes left their laser-like focus of her lips, scanning out to see all of her and all around her. His heart rate picked up as his attention caught sight of her entire face with her sealed eyes. He felt his heart would stop at any second. He saw her hair flying wildly in the wind even though the candles continued to shine without a flicker. The powerful flames left very little to the imagination as the clouds overhead parted, streaking the moonlight on top of Thya's brow like a heavenly sign.

Then he saw a hand brush across her left cheek.

It was a hand he recognized.

CHAPTER 8

Lao's body tensed as he looked at the hooded figure standing to his right in the gap beside Thya. He fixed his eyes on the hand that protruded from the sagging sleeved robe. He didn't want to look, but he couldn't turn away. The fingers looked like pale, thin leafless crooked tree branches.

He wanted to stop the madness. He wanted to end the séance. He wanted this night to vanish like it had never begun and would never happen.

The whistling had changed from a haunting melody to an ear-burning blast like a train entering a station. He wanted to cover his ears from the spine-tingling sound, but he still couldn't move.

He was afraid to look away to see if Smyrna and Phil were back into a conscious state, but he knew if they were back to their senses, they would have done something by now. He glanced over at Smyrna, but stopped halfway as he saw the shadowed figure once again.

There were two.

He turned his eyes back and watched in trepidation as the nearest hooded figure leaned over Thya as if whistling into her ear. The figure's robe tossed and swayed like Thya's hair, but Lao still couldn't feel the wind. He looked past his girlfriend to the trees in the distance, standing still. They were motionless even though it looked like a hurricane of gale force winds were blasting the circle.

The light from the moon continued to reflect onto the circle with brilliance as if it were noon. Lao could see the tiniest details down to the tattered frayed edges of the visitor's black sleeve. He continued to stare even though he didn't want to look, but he couldn't close his eyes or turn his head. It was like he was being forced to watch.

He was fighting within himself to shake free.

He was screaming in his mind, trying to undo the paralysis to help.

"Thya," he fragilely croaked, the sound unrecognizable to anyone nearby.

But one person heard it.

The hooded figure slowly turned around. Its right hand continued to caress Thya's cheek as if keeping a reign on her.

Lao's heart dropped as he watched the figure's head shift its attention to him. Lao's insides flinched as the blare of the whistle almost knocked him over. He didn't think the sound could get any more deafening, but he was wrong.

The robed figure continued to twist its neck and look down until he was facing Lao.

Lao's stomach leapt up into his throat as he looked into the face of this beast. It wasn't a face of anything he had seen, which caused a tidal wave of epic proportions crashing onto his side. He felt the wrath and unrelentless rage hit him with destructive power that would have toppled over the sturdiest of trees with its roots buried deep into the trenches of the earth.

A pale gray glow illuminated inside the features that had five dark open circles around the edges with a large red circle in the middle that shone like fire. Lao stared at the five circles that appeared like eyeless sockets positioned like a five-pointed star.

The thing reached down its left hand and touched Lao's chest.

Lao screamed in his head at the horrific pain as it felt like the creature was digging through his flesh to get to his insides. The figure continued to stoop down, lowering his head as if getting a better view of Lao. Lao looked into its face as the five dark circles changed from bottomless pits to mirrors of Lao's reactions. He saw the fear in his own eyes.

The hooded figure moved closer to Lao as its arm continued to move deeper into his chest. The reflective face and burning red light inched forward to his own. He didn't know what a possession felt like, but he knew he was being taken over.

His memory of the night before flashed as he felt like the sacrificial lamb. His grandmother had always warned him not to play with witchcraft or devil games, but he thought it was a crock of bull.

Now he wished he had listened.

His memory faded as the searing pain struck his heart. His eyes widened as he saw the hooded figure's face about to touch his. Its eyes showcased Lao's. Lao knew what was about to happen and he couldn't stop it. He was witnessing his own abduction and couldn't defend himself at all.

His insides felt on fire.

He watched as his reflection in the hood darkened, as a heavy darkness surrounded his vision. A freezing cold bath hit his face and quickly devoured the heat inside his chest. It was a cold like he had never experienced, and it stung more than the fire. It felt like knives were stabbing inside every inch of his body, as if the warm blood in his veins had thickened to sharp, pointy icicles.

The darkness passed, and he found himself once again in the circle able to see his surroundings.

But he was no longer sitting where he was a moment ago.

He was now standing.

Standing in the spot the hooded figure had been.

He looked to his right and noticed there was still a hand on Thya's cheek.

But it wasn't the whistler's.

It was his.

CHAPTER 9

Lao pulled his arm back, trying to remove his hand from her cheek, but he couldn't. It was as if they were glued, a supernatural bond sealing them together. He glanced around the group, still in their spellbound trance.

"Get out of me!" he yearned to say but couldn't force the words to escape his mouth. His tongue laid like a dead mutt in his mouth. He tried and he tried, but he couldn't do anything but moan. "Get out of me!"

He continued to say those four words to himself, telling the thing inside him to leave. He was still in control, but he wasn't sure how much longer he would be. Still, he knew the more he thought, the better he would be. Or so he hoped.

Lao looked at Thya who looked fragile, yet hard as concrete at the same time. She looked terrified with her manic convulsive appearance, yet she had unflinching reserve.

"Get out of me!" he pleaded once again, but this time, his mouth let out some air.

His eyes widened in shock.

"Ge...of...e!" he launched out as his tightening abs heaved from the static strain.

He felt a swirling of heat once again in his core as the freezing cold started to melt.

"Get out," he moaned fiercely even though it sounded like a pitiful kitten's meow.

Sweat built along his hairline, dripping onto his sweatshirt as the hoodie blotched from the dampness.

He closed his eyes and reached deep into his gut. "Get out of me!" he roared with utmost contempt. "Get out! Get out! Get out!" The last two words remained in the air as long as his lungs allowed.

He felt a rumbling in his chest, fighting and colliding against his ribs. He opened his mouth and let out a scream of pain. He felt something more than air leaving his mouth, a gray slime oozed out of his mouth. His eyes shot open, stricken in fear, as he kept his mouth wide open.

The gray gunk fell onto his shoulder and slithered across his arm. It climbed down to his elbow like a snake with its tail in his mouth. He wanted to bite down and kill whatever was in him, but he first wanted to get it all out.

He spread his mouth further apart as he felt the gooey creature drip from his quivering lip. His gag reflex was going into overdrive, but it didn't cause the thing to leave any quicker. It slowly slinked out of his mouth like an injured animal.

The gray creature continued to scoot down his arm, and he felt the coldness reach the open skin of his hand. It stopped crawling and looked behind as if waiting for the rest of it to catch up.

But Lao sensed it was looking at him for another reason.

It was as if it was saying, *Can't beat me from inside her.*

"No!" Lao screamed with his mouth still full of the tail-end of the giant slug.

He wanted to stop it, but he couldn't move. He was still stuck to Thya. Even though he wasn't gripping her, his fingers barely touched her cheekbone. He was pulling with all of his might, hoping to break the connection. Yet that brief contact was enough for the gray creature to make its way to her.

"Thya!" he screamed as the gray slime touched her skin. That split-second touch freed him from her.

He wasn't expecting to be freed from the bondage that quickly. He tried to step back and catch himself from falling, but he couldn't in time.

He screamed out, "Thya!"

She didn't respond as the gray snakelike form entered her mouth.

He watched in agony as he fell in a weightless space. He didn't care about falling. The hard ground was nothing compared to the pain Thya was enduring.

He watched in slow motion as his body came closer to the ground, but all he could see was his girlfriend. As the tail-end of the gray monster snuck itself into her mouth, he felt his heart plummet. He knew he couldn't stop it, but he quickly thought of what he could do to get it out of her.

He got it out of himself, so he could get it out of her too.

That's when he felt it. His head hit the ground, causing a sudden feeling of whiplash. He looked over as his vision blurred. Ambrose Lunderbrooke's name on his gravestone was the last thing he saw.

CHAPTER 10

"Lao. Lao," he heard, slowly opening his eyes. "Are you all right?"

Fear surged through him as a shadowed figure was kneeling over him. His eyes snapped wide open as his adrenaline pumped in attack mode. He swung his arms, reaching for the neck of the shadowed creature.

"Lao," a male's voice said. "It's me. Phil."

Lao's arms flexed and tightened as he tried to jar himself awake.

"Where's Thya?" He opened his eyes anxiously looking around, rising his back from the cold, hard ground.

"I'm right here, babe," she assured, on the other side of him, brushing his wet hair back. "You really freaked us out."

"I had you freaked out?" He grabbed her hand, kissing her palm. She laughed at the tickle of his lips on her cold hand.

"Yeah, when you fell back, we thought you had passed out or something," Smyrna expressed sitting on a nearby gravestone.

"Passed out?" he asked shocked. "I didn't pass out. Did you see it?"

The three of them looked at one another in confusion as Phil asked, "See what?"

"That..." Lao started as he tried to figure out the right words. "That gray thing that went into me and then into you." He stared into Thya's eyes as she gave a concerned look.

Phil laughed uncontrollably as Thya continued to wipe Lao's hair.

"There wasn't a gray thing," Phil snorted condescendingly.

"I know what I saw," Lao rebutted.

"Here, babe," Thya said, popping off a bottle cap, brushing his head once again. "Take a swig."

"I don't need a drink," he said, waving off the beer as she took a sip. "I know what I saw."

33

"What did you see?" Thya asked compassionately as she handed the bottle to Smyrna.

"I told you," Lao raked his fingers on the wool blanket as he looked into her eyes. "How are *you* feeling?"

"I feel fine," she said with a twisted smile and a questioning look. "Here, come on." She grabbed his arm to lift him up.

"No, really," he said, stopping as he was sitting up. "Are you burning inside or freezing?"

Thya looked at Phil, but he didn't know what to say, shrugging his shoulders as Smyrna interjected.

"Lao, you started going spastic and fell back shortly after I lit the candles."

"Huh?"

"Yeah, we thought you had a convulsion because you were shaking on the ground." Phil stood up mimicking Lao's episode. "You looked like a nut squirming on the ground."

"Phil," Thya reprimanded. "I was worried about you, but then you started to breathe normally. You were only out for a minute or two."

"What?" Lao asked as he shook his head, rubbing at a tender spot on the back of it.

"Dude," Phil said annoyed, "you're fine. Come on, get up and let's get on with it."

"Get on with it?" Lao asked as he looked over at the candles still lit on the tombstone.

"We can do this another night," Thya reasoned, squeezing Lao's hand encouragingly. "Tomorrow."

"But tonight is O'Hallow's Eve," Phil mouthed disgruntled, kicking a tombstone.

"Really?" Thya retorted with an eye roll. "I think the spirits will wait another night for us."

Phil looked over at Smyrna who nodded her head. "It's fine, Phil. Really."

Phil huffed and looked at the two women. "Fine." He leaned over the candles and blew them out in one huff.

"It's fine, Lao," Thya assured nuzzling her head on his shoulder.

"Are you really okay?" he asked again.

She smiled and nodded her head. "That was some dream you must have been having."

He looked into her eyes and then stared off into the distance as something caught his attention.

"Yeah," he said seeing a shadowed figure leaning against the church. "Just a crazy dream."

CHAPTER 11

Lao shakily stood up, partially leaning on Thya. He straightened himself up and let go of his human crutch.

"Are you feeling okay?"

He looked past her to see the shadowed figure leaning against one of the chapel's stained-glass windows.

She turned around to see what he was looking at and quickly turned back around.

He read her expression.

She saw nothing.

"I'll be fine," he assured taking a couple of steps.

"Okay. I'm going to help pick up so we can leave." Thya bent down to pick up the blanket Lao was sitting on.

"I'm going to go take a leak," he said, turning around and heading toward a tree behind the last row of gravestones in the small chapel graveyard.

"Be careful," she said as she turned her back and folded the wool blanket.

Lao stepped away, strolling through the grounds of concrete angels and cross styled headstones. The sky quickly became overcast with low-hanging clouds. The light from the moon quickly depleted until he could barely see his hand at his waist. He walked carefully, trying to watch out for tripping hazard tombstones. He shuffled his feet when he heard something familiar.

His heart rate beat with the rhythm of the melody. Fear dashed through his body as he was afraid of wetting himself. He looked around and he couldn't see anything under the shadows of the clouds. He quickly unzipped and pissed. He didn't care that his urine was probably hitting somebody's gravestone. He just wanted to take care of his business and get back to the others.

He continued to hear the whistling, but it didn't seem close. He kept watch over the grounds like a soldier, turning his neck from shoulder to shoulder to see in all directions. When he finished, he zipped himself up and turned as the clouds parted overhead.

He could see the whistler leaning against a tall statue in the middle of the graveyard, about three rows ahead.

Lao took off running toward the church. He had his path in sight. Suddenly the clouds shifted and the midnight black took over. He kept running. He remembered the gravesites' locations and took another large stride as the moon's light shone down onto his path, highlighting a tombstone in front of his face.

He tried to dart around it, but his right foot caught the corner of the stone.

He started to fall as he saw the shadowed figure heading his direction from the left, four gravesites away. His eyes widened as they fixated on the grim sight of the shadowed creature hovering toward him. He watched with fear, noticing the figure wasn't touching the ground.

He knew the ground would hit him soon, but he couldn't take his eyes off of the robed figure. He couldn't look away. Even to see the ground an inch from his face.

He opened his mouth to scream, but it was too late.

His hands hit the ground. His head hit something else.

Everything went black.

CHAPTER 12

Lao quickly stood up. He looked to his left and saw the shadowed figure hovering two tombstones away.

But it wasn't moving anymore.

Lao didn't wait around to see what would happen. The light from the moon was shining brightly, breaking through the clouds, allowing him to see his surroundings. He jumped over a small headstone and took off running to his three friends standing along the stained-glass windows on the side of the church.

Lao turned his head to see the shadowed figure in the distance. It wasn't chasing him anymore, and his heart was no longer pounding in fear. He didn't feel the burn in his lungs trying to catch his stolen breath.

In fact, he felt unusually calm.

"Slow down, pal," Phil spouted as Lao came upon them. "Who's chasing you?" he laughed as he turned to walk down the path to leave the country church.

"You okay?" Thya grabbed Lao's hand, pulling him to follow the rest of the gang. "Your hand is dirty," she pointed out with a laugh, removing her fingers from his and rubbing them on his sweatshirt.

"Oh, sorry." Lao wiped his hands nervously on his blue jeans, craning his neck to watch their backs.

"It's no biggie," she reiterated, hooking her elbow into his. "We can walk like this instead."

Lao nodded.

The sky seemed cloudless as the stars poked through the blackness. Smyrna pointed out the astrological constellations as Lao looked behind to find something else.

The shadowed figure was nowhere to be found.

Phil opened the trunk of his Volkswagen Jetta so Thya and Smyrna could toss their blankets and belongings into the back. Lao stood behind and continued to watch into the distance for his visitor to reappear. But he never showed himself.

"Lao," Thya said as she lifted her hand to his right forehead. "You're bleeding."

"I'm what?" he asked as he felt along his head to find the cut. He looked at his red fingers in shock. "I fell back there, but I didn't know I did that." He took his sleeve and wiped down his forehead, leaving his gray sweatshirt with a new red stain.

Thya reached up and felt the wound. "I think it stopped," she said as he looked at her fingers that were not red. "That was fast."

"It must have been just a scratch." Lao shrugged off the concern. He had something more sinister to think about. "I'm fine."

"See, Thya," Phil jeered a little annoyed. "He says he's fine. Come on, let's go."

The four of them piled into the four-door coupe and buckled in. Phil turned on his lights that lit up the front of the old, country church. Lao looked from the backseat with Thya by his side, scanning the grounds for anything that looked suspicious. But he found nothing out of the ordinary.

That was what concerned him the most.

CHAPTER 13

The four drove along State Route 118, a country road that connected Sardis with the small neighboring town of Modos with a population of 66 residents.

"Hey, get me another one," Phil said to Smyrna who reached down to the floorboard and unscrewed his lukewarm bottle. He guzzled the beer like water, draining the bottle in one long swig.

"Are you sure about that?" Thya squeezed Lao's hand for reassurance. He looked at her and wrapped his powerful arms around her.

"I'll keep you safe," he whispered in her ear as he leaned in for a kiss.

"I bet you will," she smiled seductively as her hand broke free from his fingers and started feeling his lean, swimmer's torso through his bulky sweatshirt.

"I think we are going to have to crack a window," Smyrna joked with a giggle, turning around to find the two in a lovers' pose. She looked at Phil who winked back at her. She reached her hand and placed it on his thigh, playfully inching it higher up his leg until she found what she was looking for. She didn't want him to feel neglected.

He closed his eyes to enjoy her touch as his headlights reflected the taillights of a car ahead of them on the side of the road. He briefly opened his eyes, reminding himself he was still the driver and needed to stay alert.

He swerved to the left, giving the deserted truck ample room since its flat back left tire was over the line.

"Whoa." Thya slid in the backseat, landing in Lao's lap. But he didn't mind.

"Moron," Phil huffed under his breath as he passed.

"What happened?" Lao looked out the window as Thya continued to nibble on his neck. His eyes locked onto a gray figure moving on the side of the road.

Phil turned his head. "Some fool didn't pull all the way off the road."

"I think we just passed the fool," Lao grinned as he turned around to see the figure slowly moving up the road.

"What are you looking at?" Thya asked, touching his chin, maneuvering it to meet her lips once again.

"Don't be making any babies in my backseat," Phil laughed as he watched the two in his rearview mirror.

"Phil!" Smyrna screamed at the top of her lungs.

Phil refocused his vision onto the road as a glimpse of a dark, brown silhouette appeared in a flash. He gripped the wheel and quickly swerved, but he still caught its backside on his front right bumper.

He slammed on his brakes as his tires squealed and smoked. He went from 85 miles per hour to stopping in six seconds, causing a couple of bottles to smash on the floorboard and the aroma of beer to fill the car.

"What was that?" Phil asked, turning to Smyrna panting with her eyes closed.

"I think it was a deer. I didn't get a good look, but I could see something dark moving along the side of the road."

"A deer?" Phil asked.

"Do you think we better go check it out?" Lao asked.

"What if it's injured?" Thya commented.

"What are we going to do, Thya?" Phil bellowed slamming his fist on his car horn. "Put it in the trunk and take it to a vet?" he mocked with disdain as he twisted his neck to see her expression. "It's a freakin' deer. There are thousands of them out here."

"I don't know," she softly responded as she sunk into the dark confines of the backseat.

Phil opened his door and Lao followed. The two went around to the front bumper and examined the dent and embedded scratches with the flashlights on their phones.

"My parents are going to be pissed!" Phil shouted, kicking the rocks on the side of the road.

"It was an accident," Lao countered encouragingly. "It could have happened to anyone."

"Yeah, if only I hadn't lied to my parents about where I was going tonight," he groaned in disgust. "I'm supposed to be a few blocks from my house studying at Smyrna's house." He stopped and raised his fists to the sky. "Not in this Godforsaken part of the county."

"They'll understand," Lao appealed as he stood still, listening. He thought he heard a faint sound in the distance.

"My parents are religious nuts," he spit out. "They told me to not be on the roads on Halloween because they feel it isn't safe to be out with," he stopped and looked up at the sky, "all the crazies that are making a muck on the devil's holiday."

"It's going to be okay," Lao repeated compassionately.

"No, man, you don't understand," Phil exploded. "I'm going to be grounded for a month. My folks are bat-eyed crazy. The only time they are going to let me out of the house is to go to their brainwashing church four times a week."

Lao didn't know what to say. He had never been fond of Phil, and this conversation wasn't bringing them any closer.

"Come on," Phil barked stomping away from the headlights.

Lao stood beside his unopened door. He could faintly hear something moaning in pain. He knew it wasn't Phil griping about the spilt beer on his floor mats that was going to tack on another month of punishment.

Lao looked into the grass but couldn't see anything. He thought he knew what the sound was. He had heard the dying deer.

CHAPTER 14

Phil and Smyrna dropped off Lao after taking Thya home. Lao walked through the desolate apartment parking lot to get to his building. He pulled out his phone and checked his messages. Thya hadn't replied yet.

When he unlocked the door, the grate of the lock announced to anyone awake he was home. He found his mom snoozing on the couch with a half-drunk bottle of red wine straddled between her legs.

"I'm home," he whispered sarcastically walking through the living room toward his bedroom.

He quickly undressed, throwing his sweatshirt and jeans in the hamper as he walked around in his American Eagle boxer briefs. Looking in the mirror he caught sight of the gash on the right side of his forehead. He touched the wound but didn't feel any pain. There was no blood trickling down, just an open cut. Many times, his mother had stitched him up so they didn't have to have an emergency room bill. He thought she could help him again.

Tomorrow.

He didn't want her drunk hands getting that close to his face with a sharp needle.

Thya finally responded with a seductive text image of her in her bra. *Sweet dreams.*

He smiled at the little game they played. He turned his back to his mirror and positioned the camera over his shoulder to take a picture of his backside. He gripped his left thumb into his waistband and let his underwear fall to the ground. He snapped a picture.

He examined the portrait and thought he looked good enough to share. He sent the scandalous nude with the same *Sweet dreams* message before throwing his phone on his bed.

He bent down to pick up his underwear and put them back on. Standing in front of his mirror, he flexed, realizing a minute too late he should have flexed his butt muscles in the photo he sent.

His bed welcomed him, but he wasn't tired. He reclined on top of the sheets and scrolled through his Instagram feed, liking the photos that caused him to take a second glance. He noticed the time on his phone, 1:42 a.m., but he still wasn't tired.

He knew 5:30 was going to be here soon, and he needed to get some sleep so he could make it for his early morning swim team practice. He laid his phone on his nightstand beside his alarm clock.

He closed his eyes and waited.

And waited.

And waited some more.

He thought he would eventually drift to sleep, but his eyes were not getting heavy. His alarm clock signaled 3:33 a.m. with a neon green glow.

Fluffing his pillow, he tossed and rolled over to his side. He closed his eyes again, but instead of falling asleep, he fell into a nighttime daydream.

CHAPTER 15

Lao found himself walking down a deserted country road. An intersection formed and a road sign for State Route 118 reflected under a full moon. He turned left and started walking the lone straightaway until a worn-out metal mailbox with 1260 in silver numbers down the wooden post urged him to turn. A white stone path led him to an archway with two olive trees as its base, one on each side of the path. Their branches stretched, meeting and tethered together by a rusted chain in the middle above the path. A wooden board swinging overhead dangled from the chain like a pendulum, swinging back and forth in the wind. Pergamum Farm was painted like a child had written it in white lettering, off center and slanted upwards.

He proceeded further up the path as the white stones became a dirt path that separated toiled ground that looked barren and unforgiving. For miles on both sides of the path no crops could be seen on the farmland. It looked like a vacant lot where a farmer used to live.

The road forked straight ahead. On one side, a plantation-style house rose above the unfertile ground on top of a hill; the other side darted left into a shady tree-lined path. He went left and walked under the branches that eclipsed the moon's light, listening to the stillness. His nostrils tingled from the lack of smell of fresh manure beyond the trees.

The trees broke way into a clearing with an old, rickety barn with missing boards on the side leaving nothing hidden behind the walls. He stood outside and poked his head through one of the many missing panels. Bales of hay lined the inside like rows of auditorium seating as candles illuminated the aisle down the middle, walkways, and ends. Six thumps broke through the silence.

Then suddenly, his daydream went into reverse. He walked backwards to the path leading him away from the barn to the small area of trees. He walked through the blackness until the moon's light illuminated showcasing the house up on the hill. He continued to walk backwards on the dirt path and then the stone path, past the entryway with the Pergamum Farms sign. He turned back onto the paved state route and walked backwards until his daydream ended.

He looked at his clock.

3:34 a.m.

CHAPTER 16

Lao grabbed his towel hanging in his locker as he proceeded with the rest of the men's swim team to the fifty meters pool to get some early morning laps before school. He passed the mirror and noticed the wound on his head looked the same as it had last night.

Coach Haman was waiting beside the pool for the team with his clipboard in hand to assign their lanes and partners for the warm-up exercises.

Lao partnered up with Hector as they both dove into the pool to get acclimated to the chill of the water.

"Did they forget and turn off the heater last night?" Hector yelled as he popped his head up from under the water.

"Feels fine to me," Lao grinned, doing his kicking exercises along the pool's edge.

The fifteen swimmers stretched and warmed up their arms and legs with a few relaxing laps up and down the pool.

The whistle blew and each swimmer stopped and waited for Coach Haman's command.

"Get to your starting blocks!" he shouted. "Boys freestyle two-hundred meters first and then girls!" Each swimmer swam to the nearest edge and exited the pool.

Lao stood on the starting block in lane two since they were assigned their positions by the season's stats: the closer to the center lane, the better. Since he was in lane two, he was usually in the bottom half. He assumed the starting position like the rest of the guys in his navy Nike Jammer shorts. He crouched down, slightly bent his knees, gripped the starting block with his fingers, and waited for the coach to blow the whistle for the swimmers to dive in.

"On your mark! Get set!" Coach Haman shouted then blew his whistle.

Lao jumped from the starting block, flying toward the water as he pierced the surface with a clean dive. He kept his body straight and started his dolphin kicks to gain some momentum before rising to the surface. He started his freestyle stroke and kick, his arms and legs exhibiting beautiful form. His head rested above the water, keeping watch on his closest competitors through his blue Speedo goggles.

He was outpacing the swimmers in lanes one and three, but knew that a win was most likely not going to happen.

He reached the end of the first lap and completed his tumble turn, pressing off the side of the wall with his legs, which ricocheted him under the water. He dolphin kicked for a little while and then reached the surface and started his strokes and kicks. His heart was usually beating during a race, but his heart rate was unbelievably low for him. Lao continued to push himself in his newfound stamina as he broke away from the swimmers in lane one and three. He completed his second lap and once again did a front somersault and tumble turn. He was halfway done.

He usually would feel a burn in his legs by now, which would cause his pace to slow, but there wasn't a burn. He felt relaxed and comfortable. He reached the end of his third lap and proceeded back to the starting point of the race to conclude the last fifty meters. He rose from his dolphin kick and was startled when he actually passed the swimmer in line one who hadn't even finished his third lap yet.

He searched for some stamina for the hardest part of the race as he kicked and stroked as if he were being chased by a shark. He looked toward the center lanes of the pool and wondered how off pace he was from the fastest on the team, but he couldn't see them ahead of him. He saw the change in the pool lane dividers signaling to him he had ten meters left.

He gave it his all. He took a couple more long strokes and powerful kicks and reached his hand forward to touch the side of the pool. He raised his head from under the water and looked toward the center of the pool where Coach Haman usually stood to call out people's time.

But Coach Haman wasn't standing at lane four.

Lao reached his hand onto the pool's edge to look around. But he was confused. All the guys were still swimming toward him.

"Lao!" Coach Haman screamed with his stopwatch in his hand.

Lao looked up, surprised to see the man standing over his starting block.

"You just broke the school record!" he beamed with uncontained excitement. "What did you have for breakfast this morning to make you do that?"

"Uh," Lao said without any lost breath and confusion in his voice. "Nothing."

"You know what this means?" Coach Haman asked flabbergasted.

Lao shook his head no, still in a state of shock as he watched a few of the guys finally stop their race.

"If you can do this during the meet, you'll be heading to state," Coach Haman hailed still looking at the stopwatch in amazement. "State!"

CHAPTER 17

Lao stood in the boy's locker room and dropped his towel from around his waist to put on his dry clothes. He pulled on his pants and stood shirtless, examining his forehead cut. His ears perked as he heard a familiar sound.

He turned around, looking for where the whistling was coming from. He saw nothing to alarm him, but the sound was getting louder. "Where are you?" he asked softly, scanning the room for a gray figure, but there was another aisle of lockers behind him. He walked away to search the rest of the room, but the whistling seemed to be at his back.

He turned quickly with fists ready to punch.

"Oh!" Lao shouted, startled as Reid walked up beside him drying off thinking he was the last one left in the shower. "It's you."

"Good race," Reid walked two lockers down with his towel wrapped around his lean waist, unaware of Lao's fighting stance.

"You too."

"Nah." Reid shook his head as he tossed his towel aside and started dressing. He looked over at Lao who was oblivious to his staring. "I don't want to sound rude..." he started before Lao finished his statement.

"How'd I beat you?" he asked with a wide-eyed expression. He shrugged his shoulders and then pulled on his gray school t-shirt and Nike hoodie. He grabbed his backpack hanging on a hook in his locker. "I wish I knew."

Reid didn't believe that explanation by his cocked-eye look and furrowed brow.

"It's true," Lao offered shutting his locker and spinning the combination wheel.

"If you know something I can do to help with my speed," he stopped and zipped up his blue jeans, "you would help me out, right?"

Lao quickly shook his head. "I didn't take anything."

"No. No," Reid responded defensively. "I'm not saying you're doing anything illegal." He stopped and pulled out his shirt from the shelf in his locker. "But if you find, you know, something that could help the team out, you would tell us, right?"

"But I didn't! Promise. I just beat you fair and square."

"Come on," Reid said with a laugh. "I've always beaten you, and then the week of our last match, you come up and swim like that," he said pointing at the pool. "I've never seen Haman look like that."

"Like what?" Lao puffed his chest taking a step closer to the accuser.

"You know," Reid said pulling on his shirt.

"No, I don't. Why don't you tell me?"

Reid looked at Lao and patted him on his shoulder. "How does the guy one level above being the team's towel boy swim like that?"

Lao's eyes burned with rage as his nostrils flared. He looked at Reid and wanted to say something, but didn't. He turned and walked away.

"You weren't even out of breath after any of the races, Lao!" Reid shouted as Lao started toward the door.

Lao stopped and turned to look at Reid who was tucking in his shirt. "You're just mad because you're not the star anymore."

"And why is that?" Reid asked under his breath as he stooped down to tie his sneakers.

CHAPTER 18

Lao went through the morning in a state of unrest. He had never noticed how many people whistled. He found whistlers at the urinals. He discovered whistlers in the cafeteria waiting in line for their sliced peaches. He could even hear a few stragglers whistling in the hallways between classes. It seemed like wherever he went, the sound of a whistle was nearby. He tried different ways of canceling out the sound, but it always returned.

Louder and clearer.

"Hey, babe," Thya said as she sat down beside Lao with her tray of pizza and salad. "How's your head?"

"It's fine." He rubbed his gash and didn't feel the pain with one hand as he scooted his salad around with his fork with the other.

"It doesn't look fine," she suggested taking a bite. "You may need to have someone look at it."

"Nah." He looked over at her and shrugged off her concern. "It's not bleeding, and I don't even feel it."

"If you say so," she said with an odd look as Smyrna and Phil sat down with their food trays. "Glad to see you're still alive."

"Yeah," Phil said with an unconvincing smile. "I guess you can call it that."

"He's grounded," Smyrna interjected, opening her bottle of water.

"Too bad," Lao said aloof as he folded his arms.

"Not hungry?" Thya asked as she took another bite of her pizza.

"I just don't have an appetite," he said as his ears picked up that frightening sound. "Do you hear that?"

The three friends looked around the table confused. "Hear what?" Phil asked as he looked at Thya for reassurance. She shrugged her shoulders and echoed his question.

"That whistling." Lao raked his fingers through his short hair, looking around the cafeteria for the whistler.

The three of them looked at one another before all turning to Lao.

"Don't tell me you don't hear that?" Lao asked flabbergasted.

"Maybe when you hit your head, you got a concussion or something," Smyrna said as Thya nodded her head in agreement.

"Yeah, babe," she said, wrapping her arms around Lao's body. "Maybe you need to get it checked out."

"I don't have a concussion. My head feels fine."

"Well, why don't you eat something?" Thya said positively.

"I don't want to eat." Lao huffed in aggravation pushing away his tray. He clasped his hands over his ears and laid his head on the table. "I just want the whistling to stop."

Thya rubbed Lao's back, inching her fingers up to his hairline on his neck. "I hear it now," she said as she looked at her friends across the table, begging them to acknowledge the sound.

"Yeah," Smyrna said unconvincingly. "I'm hearing it."

"I can't hear anything," Phil said before Smyrna kicked him under the table. "What?" he hissed, rubbing his shin. "I can't."

Smyrna turned her head to Phil and gave him a look to just pretend. He shook his head as he stuck a fork in his pizza.

"Lao," Thya leaned her head down smelling the remnants of chlorine in his hair. "Are you okay?"

CHAPTER 19

Lunch ended and the four departed in different directions. Lao trudged through the noisy hallways with his U.S. history textbook in his backpack. The whistling had subsided, but he wasn't sure it vanished. The sound of slamming lockers, loud conversations, and squeaky sneakers on the newly mopped floor drowned out everything else.

He passed Mr. Pruitt's biology classroom with croaking frogs and the relaxing sound of bubbling water from his aquarium. A funny feeling hit Lao causing him to glance toward the end of the hallway.

He didn't hear the whistler.

He saw it.

He stopped, causing a collision of students behind him, pressing on his back and yelling for him to continue. But he couldn't. He didn't want to move any closer. The whistler stood motionless, as if staring into Lao's soul as the mass of students unconsciously followed its orders and parted down the middle. The two stared at one another as a student from behind pushed past Lao, causing the trance to be broken.

Lao blinked and stepped out of the middle of the hallway. He stared at a stranger's locker, number 813 wondering if the whistler was still there. Suddenly a great whistle sounded, and the students scurried to their next room.

He tentatively looked over his shoulder at the end of the hall. A feeling of safety washed over him as the whistler had disappeared.

Lao quickly followed the herd of students to reach his next class.

"Laonardo," Mrs. Winters said as he nodded and entered her room with historical posters of the Bill of Rights, the Constitution, and the Declaration of Independence plastered on her walls.

He sat down at his desk beside the window that overlooked the neatly maintained grounds of the high school. All the leaves that had fallen over the weekend were already raked and tied up in big black bags scattered around the grounds like barracks of a game of paintball. He admired the foliage from this vantage point. The reddening leaves clung to the tree limbs, showing off their beauty like a pageant contestant.

The bell chimed one final time, signaling the start of the next class.

But as the bell ended another sound started.

Lao froze in his seat with his hands pressed against the wooden desktop, his fingers suctioned onto the surface. Mrs. Winters started her lecture, commanding the class to open their textbooks, but Lao couldn't hear a word. The whistling sound overrode everything else.

He turned his head and watched everyone get out their textbooks and pencils. The more he turned his head, the louder the deafening sound filled his ears. He didn't want to look around the room, but he couldn't stop.

A darkness grew out of the back corner, ebbing its way across the sunlit room. He felt it hovering over him like a cruel fog. He turned his head to the corner and saw it. Standing frozen like a statue chiseled by Michelangelo with its robe that looked as soft as wool, but as still as rock. The red circle in the middle of its face blazing like a fire engulfing its being. A beam of heat hit his chest.

Slam!

He spun his head toward the window as an eagle slid down the cracking glass.

"What hit the glass?" Mrs. Winters asked as a couple of students rushed over the window.

"A big hawk or something," someone said as Lao's paralysis eased. He stood up and walked over to the window beside him that had a fresh new crack in the center. He looked past the glass and saw the flopping bird, agonizing in pain from the sudden crash.

He wanted to turn away and not watch, but he couldn't. He couldn't take his eyes off the wounded creature. He didn't want to see an animal in pain, but he couldn't look away. He wanted to close his eyes, but he had no control over his body.

It was as if he was being forced to watch the death.

The students walked away from the glass, but Lao wasn't one of them. He was glued to the pitiful sight.

"Such a pity," Mrs. Winters said walking up beside Lao, looking out the window. "To suffer such anguish, and all we can do is watch and wait."

The whistler appeared outside the glass. It looked up at Lao and then touched the head of the injured creature. The bird instantly stopped twitching. The whistling stopped and Lao could move once again, but he remained transfixed on the bird.

It was dead and the whistler was gone; the rest of the class carried on, oblivious of the robed figure that was among them.

CHAPTER 20

The school day ended as the students rushed out of their last class, sprinting to their lockers before exiting the school. Lao stood outside among a group of students waiting for the oncoming school bus with his phone in hand, texting Thya about plans for the night. She had some homework and a test to study for.

That's fine, he texted back. *Are we still on for tomorrow night?*

Yeah.

I can't believe it's been six months.

Me either, babe.

So, you want to go to the place of our first date? He grinned at the romantic gesture and waited for her response.

"I hate it when I can see my breath," she said with clattering teeth. "It's just not normal."

"Wear a jacket," an uncompassionate guy huffed from the outskirts of the circle. "It's that easy."

"But I didn't bring one," she moaned. "Does anyone have a jacket I can wear?"

No one answered.

"Lao's standing in a t-shirt and you don't hear him complaining," someone said nearby as Lao continued to look down at his unanswered text.

"Huh?" he responded as he heard his name.

Eva pointed at the hoodie tied around Lao's waist. "If you're not going to wear that, can I?" she asked, trembling and rubbing her bare arms to stay warm.

"Sure," Lao untied his sweatshirt and handed it to her. "Just give it back before you leave."

"Promise," She pulled the sweatshirt down, modeling it for anyone watching. "It's nice and toasty," she said looking at Lao invitingly.

"Glad you're enjoying it," Lao stood unfazed as he watched his phone indicate Thya was typing.

"Why did you do that?" someone harped on Eva from behind. "Taking his sweatshirt."

"He's not cold," she rebutted. "You can't even see his breath. He's fine."

So what movie are we going to see?

Movie? he texted with a laughing emoji. *That wasn't our first date.*

Well, I thought the movie was our real first date, she quickly replied.

No! It was ice cream at Frost's and then a walk around the park.

You're right! I was getting confused with when we went with Phil and Smyrna as friends.

The bus came to a stop as Lao thought back over the last year of hanging out with Thya and her friends. He didn't remember ever going to the movies with them.

Silly, he texted back before climbing up the bus steps and taking a seat near the front.

CHAPTER 21

Lao continued to text Thya on the bus ride home until she vanished into her homework. His stop was one of the last ones on the route, so he leaned his head back and stared at the metal mint green ceiling. He wasn't sleepy, but the strange occurrences through the day had caused him to feel mentally drained.

He stared at the poster of the school play from last spring, *No Exit*, and wondered when someone was finally going to take it down. He always thought it was ironic having the poster on the bus since everyone wanted to exit it as soon as possible. He counted the bolts connecting the two metal sheets above his head, holding them together with some welding magic. He counted the markings going up and down as if counting sheep. He let his mind drift into a daydream state.

He journeyed in his mind's eye to the same farm ground he saw in his quick dream last night. He made his way down the same state route, turning at the same rusted-out mailbox with a loose postal flag dangling by a single screw. The white stone path changed to a dirt one as he once again found himself at the crossroads where the road diverged. He followed the path through the darkened small forest taking him to the shabby barn looking like it needed only a good gust of wind to knock all four sides down. He inched his way closer to the barn and looked inside through a hole in the wall. He saw hay bales placed for seating as he heard a faint whistle followed by six thuds.

The journey to the barn was a gentle walk, but the journey back was a sprint. Instead of walking backwards, he ran, catching the sights from a new direction as he tried to outrun the whistling melody. Lao ran to the forest, through the darkened path, out of the woods, and back down the dirt path that changed to a stone-covered one. He reached the mailbox and turned down State Route 118.

His phone vibrated as he awoke from his daydream. 3:33 p.m. shone with a text from his mother saying she was going to be working late that night.

He didn't respond. He stuffed his phone back into his pocket and stared out the school bus window. They were traveling down a different road from their normal route.

"Mr. John," Lao said since he couldn't remember the bus driver's last name, "where are we going?"

"There's a detour for some road construction," he said behind the steering wheel as the school bus sped along the two-lane country road. "You'll get home soon enough."

Lao looked out the window and something caught his eye. It was a dead deer on the side of the road that looked mutilated and devoured by birds of prey. He wanted to look away at the animal with its tongue drooping from its open mouth, but something inside urged him to look closer.

The bus sped by as he saw a large clearing of land with nothing growing. A sign at the entrance matched the one he had visioned twice in the last twelve hours.

Pergamum Farm.

"Mr. John," Lao said as he looked out the window, straightening up and alert. He saw all the details of his dream. The mailbox, the sign, the path, and the farmhouse on the hill. "Where are we?"

John looked up into his large rearview mirror, "I think we are on State Route 118," he said after he thought for a second. "Yeah, I think that's it."

Lao looked out the window, straining his neck to see the farm they just passed as he felt a wave of concern.

"Deer!"

A whistle sound commingled with the squealing of the bus's brakes alerted Lao that something was about to happen.

CHAPTER 22

John parked the bus and jumped out the door. Lao sat in his seat, clutching both ears with his hands to drown out the whistling seeping through cracked windows.

John rushed back on the bus and spoke into his two-way radio. He was speaking fast, looking out the window and periodically in the rearview mirror to check on the students before jumping out again.

Lao looked around and noticed most of the students couldn't care less. He stood up and felt a gravitational pull to the other side of the bus to look out the window, but he couldn't see anything except John looking down at the pavement in front of the school bus.

Curiosity got the better of Lao as he stepped away from the seat to look out the windshield. He peered over the edge of the bus's orange hood and saw two pairs of brown, furry legs. He still couldn't see everything, so he slowly stepped down through the open door. He felt his legs hit the concrete and stepped around to the front of the bus. The whistling was agonizing, but he couldn't stop. He felt a darkness invade and stepped forward to see the lame animal. The deer's head moved and locked eyes with Lao.

He felt compassion for the beautiful deer, but compassion quickly turned to fear as a long, loud whistle almost caused Lao's knees to weaken. Lao froze as John's body moved, motioning for him to return to the bus, but he couldn't move. He watched statuesque as the whistler passed by, his robe brushing by his shoulder as the touch of his cloth burned a freezing chill to his core.

Lao wanted to let out a scream for pain, a yell for warning, a shrill for fear, but all he could do was remain still with his unblinking eyes watching and waiting.

The whistler approached the deer and leaned down. He looked up at Lao as the red, fiery light in the middle of its face went out causing a darkness, like a bottomless pit. Lao's eyes widened, even though he wanted to look away. The whistler touched the deer between the eyes, causing the twitching animal to cease.

In an instant the darkness disappeared and the whistling ceased.

"Well, are you going to help me move it?" John asked as he picked up the front two legs.

Lao felt movement once again in his body and stepped toward the dead animal. He felt remorse, but mostly he felt like he was doing something wrong.

They pulled the dead animal to the side of the road and dropped it along the grass.

"What now?"

"What do you mean?" John asked walking back to the bus.

"Aren't we going to do something?"

"It's dead, Lao," John asked unconcerned. "There's nothing else to do."

Lao stood by the dead deer. He wanted to bend down and feel the fur as if to soothe the dead creature. But John was right. It was dead, and there was nothing else he could do.

Petting the fur wouldn't soothe the deer.

But maybe it would have soothed Lao.

CHAPTER 23

Lao entered his empty apartment and tossed his backpack on the chair at his computer desk. He flipped on the television, but nothing caught his attention. He kept it on anyway and started his algebra homework. After thirty minutes of problems with letters and numbers, he finished his assignment. He had eaten nothing all day, but he still didn't feel hungry.

He went to the kitchen and fixed a bowl of cereal and forced a few bites before dumping the rest of his sugary cornflakes down the garbage disposal.

He texted a couple of his swim team friends, but no one responded. He wondered if Reid had already started sabotaging his inner circle and a surge of anger rose.

Hey man, I took nothing. I don't use drugs or steroids, he texted. He watched as his message went from delivered to read. He waited for Reid to respond, but he never did.

What? You don't feel like accusing me of anything now? Lao once again waited for Reid's response.

Once again that was all he did—wait.

Lao grabbed his barbells under his bed and started doing some bicep curls. He didn't want this morning's show to be a fluke. He wanted to show the team he could do it again.

He dropped the weights and started doing some push-ups. He usually did twenty-five at a time and rested for a few minutes to do another set, but he astounded himself when he reached one hundred without breaking a sweat.

He jumped up and started doing some burpees. His one-minute round lasted ten minutes.

He smiled as he took off his shirt and flexed his muscles, posing and showing off his newfound strength in the mirror as if he were Mr.

Universe. He was staring into his reflection, admiring his pecs when he noticed a shadow in the corner behind the computer desk.

His eyes widened as the shadow moved. He couldn't take his eyes off of the corner. He wanted to flee the room, but a new idea hit him, causing the fear he'd had a second ago to fade as if he'd blown out a candle.

He slowly turned around and faced the darkened corner.

"If you gave me this strength," he said as he struck a pose, popping every muscle in his upper body, "then thank you."

CHAPTER 24

The night was slow and long. Lao heard his mother come in from work sometime after nine, but she went straight to the bathroom, took a shower, and then went to bed.

Lao kept his phone at his hip on the bed, but everyone was busy or ignoring him.

He laid on his bed and kept an eye on the shadow, but it hadn't moved in the last two hours. He turned off his television and turned on the radio, not to listen to the music, but to drown out the silence.

Lao turned his attention from the shadow in the corner to his ceiling. It wasn't anything intriguing to look at, but it was a change. He lowered the volume on his music and could faintly hear a whistle.

He turned the radio off and the whistling was clearly evident, growing louder as he laid back on his pillow. He flipped on the radio and increased the volume and waited for the whistling to be overpowered.

It wasn't.

He rolled over on his side, turning his back to his room and covered his head with his pillow.

He could still hear the whistling.

He'd thought he could make the whistler his friend, but it was now clear to him the creature didn't want to be friends. He threw his pillow off of his face and rolled over.

The feeling of friendliness vanished as the whistler's face was an inch from his, lying beside him on his bed. Lao looked into the various holes on his face and felt sickened. Suddenly, fear engulfed him. He scooted back and rolled off his bed, landing on the hard floor.

When he jumped up, he found himself alone.

The shadow in the corner was gone as well.

CHAPTER 25

Lao crawled back into bed and waited for sleep to come, but his eyes wouldn't get heavy. He looked up various tips for falling asleep, and one by one he tried them, and one by one they failed.

He looked over at his alarm clock that radiated 2:05 a.m. He tossed and turned, but every time he turned his body away from the corner that housed the shadow earlier, he felt a twinge of fear. Lao rolled onto his stomach and yelled into his pillow. He was tired of not being sleepy, aggravated with the feeling of the unknown, and falling into a state of fear and dread.

He grabbed his remote control and turned on his television. He flipped through the channels until an eerie picture emerged with a time stamp of 3:33 a.m. The screen showed a night camera view of someone traveling down a little country road. The headlights shone onto a road sign, State Route 118, before turning left onto the road. It drove on the road a short distance before stopping in front of an old tree still full of leaves. The interior vehicle light showed a dangling red evergreen tree air freshener on the rearview mirror. The person got out of the car and proceeded up the road. He could hear the footsteps on the pavement. The guest turned at a mailbox marked 1260 and walked under the sign for Pergamum Farms. He trudged up the path and turned right when the path diverted into a section of trees. Soon the trees cleared and a shabby looking barn sat along the path. The person walked up to the barn and stood outside. He waited and knocked six times on the side before the door swiftly swung open. He walked into the barn as the screen went black with the time still glowing in the upper left corner.

3:33 a.m.

Lao got up and walked to his screen. He thought he could see something moving in the blackness. There was a strange sound, barely audible. He raised the volume and knelt by the television stand.

"Come," a voice whispered. "Find what you are looking for."

Lao cocked his head and leaned closer to the television.

"Lao," the voice said as if it knew it was being watched. "We are waiting."

He fell back at the sound of his name, catching himself on his elbows.

The screen changed to a night scene with a young man in the middle, standing with a school's sweatshirt with a hood over his head. Lao raised himself up and touched the screen to make sure he wasn't dreaming. He felt the static on his fingertips.

"Lao!" the boy screamed as the robed figures around him cheered.

The video footage zoomed closer to the boy's face as he took off his hood. The screen froze on his face.

He looked at the boy's right forehead. It had a cut.

Lao raised his hand and felt a gash on the same spot.

The screen went black. Lao sat there shaking on the inside as he looked into the television showing his reflection.

He was still wearing his swim team hoodie.

The same one he just saw.

CHAPTER 26

Lao lay in bed for half an hour and wondered what to do. He was even more wide awake and didn't see himself drifting to sleep anytime soon.

His car keys on the computer desk were beckoning him to pick them up and take a joyride out to the farm. He didn't want to cause his mom to worry in case she woke up and noticed her car was gone, even though he knew he could leave for a week and she wouldn't care. She would only care he took her car and was using the gas she paid for.

He put on a pair of blue jeans and grabbed his wallet, checking to make sure he had some money, just in case. He scribbled a note to his mom and laid it next to the bathroom sink.

Within five minutes of deciding to investigate the place in his visions, he was out the door.

He started her Nissan Altima and steered it through the parking lot to the road. He rolled the windows down, hoping to smell the autumn air, but he smelled nothing. He looked over at the rearview mirror and noticed his mom's red air freshener.

The same as in the video.

He didn't know if that should give him reassurance for making the right move or scared for falling into a trap. He decided not to think about it yet and concentrated on enjoying the feeling of freedom behind the steering wheel. His mom worked odd shifts at the hospital, so he rarely drove her vehicle. Occasionally on weekends she would allow him to borrow the car, but it was rare.

He went through the quiet town of Sardis and realized it was even quieter this time of night. He looked down at the clock: 2:49 a.m.

He stopped at the various streetlights and stop signs, but thought it was pointless this time of morning; he was the only one on the road. He crossed through the city to get to the countryside of Sardis, heading toward the city of Modos. He approached the intersection he had seen in his vision three times so far and turned left onto State Route 118.

He gripped the steering wheel wondering if he was making a foolish mistake. But he had a feeling he was making the right decision.

He drove along the lonely country road under the light from the moon. He almost didn't need the vehicle's headlights on this clear evening, but he kept them on just in case. He didn't want to hit a deer like Phil or the school bus. He watched on both sides of the road, making sure no deer were going to be jumping up and startling him.

In the distance he saw the outline of a tall, fully leafed tree with a little parking area in front of it. He slowed his vehicle and went off the road.

He sat in the parked car for a few minutes before turning off the ignition. Looking into the rearview mirror and noticing no one was around him, he grabbed his phone, clutching it in his hand as he opened the car door. He quietly shut it and walked up the road.

He came to the address he had seen with the old mailbox; the postal flag was squeaking as the metal scraped from the light gust of wind. He walked forward and entered Pergamum Farm.

He turned around but there was still no one to be seen.

He proceeded over the white stone path and soon went onto a dirt road. He walked up the hill and noticed the lack of vegetation growing around him. He thought maybe this was because it was harvest time and the crops had just been reaped, but he turned around and looked across the road and noticed the crops were still in that field.

He didn't have a reasonable explanation except maybe it was an abandoned farm or the owner was too old for farming. He came up with his own story as the road split in two. Looking further up the hill, he noticed a large, two-story farmhouse. He couldn't make out the details under the moonlight, but it still looked livable.

He poked his head into the small forest. He couldn't see the end, but based upon his visions, it wasn't that long of a walk. He proceeded through and felt the silence. Even the nocturnal animals were taking a break from their nighttime adventures. He looked around the scenery, but he couldn't make out much of it. The treetops had stopped the light from the moon.

He turned on his phone flashlight and scanned the area. He couldn't see much with the little light, but he could walk without tripping over fallen branches or protruding tree roots. He got through the darkest portion of the woods, and a glimmer of light shone from the exit ahead.

Lao turned off his flashlight and walked toward the light. He made it to the clearing and saw a large old barn ahead, but it didn't look like anyone was around. There weren't any vehicles or light coming from the cracks of the barn's siding. He stepped closer and came to the door.

He remembered the knock was six times.

He raised his hand and stopped as he was about to hit the wood with his first tap. He thought he heard something coming from the other side.

"Come," a sinister sounding voice said. "Find what you are looking for."

The voice sent a chill down his spine. He couldn't finish the knock.

Suddenly he found himself in a state of confusion and escalated fear. His questions rose, and his fear ignited into an explosion commanding him to run.

So he did. He turned.

That's when he heard it. He hadn't heard it all night walking through the farmland, but he heard it loud and clear.

And saw it too. The whistler was standing at the entrance of the woods.

"He's leaving!"

CHAPTER 27

"He's leaving!" a man yelled from inside the barn as the door swung open with a large creak.

"Lao!" the man shouted. "We are waiting!"

Lao froze in his tracks. He felt surrounded. On one side was the strange whistler that had been haunting him for the last couple of days, and on the other was a stranger who had been haunting him in the last hour. Both felt untrustworthy. But only one appeared human.

"Just go away!" the man shouted to the whistler. "Lao, come back!"

Lao turned his head to see a small crowd gathering behind the older man. They were all robed in similar garb, like a secret society that Phil and Smyrna only dreamed of becoming members of. The group ranged in ages from young to old with both men and women.

He didn't feel safe but felt like a monster about to be attacked.

"Come on, son." The man showed his open hands as a welcoming gesture. He took a step closer as if trying to befriend and rehabilitate a wild animal.

Lao looked back at the woods and saw the whistler. He wasn't moving or attempting to come any closer.

Lao turned his back to the group as he faintly heard the older man command the others. "Get him."

He suddenly felt not like an animal they were trying to protect, but one they wanted to cage.

So he ran.

CHAPTER 28

Lao ran away from the pack, but not toward the whistler. He sprinted toward the open field with acres of flat dirt as he regretted his decision to come to this elusive farm in the dead of night telling no one.

He looked back over his shoulder. He saw the whistler's red light under his hood standing in front of the entrance of the forest. It hadn't moved.

Lao's feet left the solid ground and entered soft, tilled soil. His speed dramatically slowed as his feet sank with every step. He felt the earth pulling him down, but he would not let it stop him. His legs still felt strong even though he was having to try twice as hard. He looked back and knew if he was having difficulty running the others would as well.

He turned his head and continued to run as a familiar sound revved through the clamor. He knew what the sound was as a light shone behind him. He tried to use the light for his advantage to watch out for divots in the dirt, but he couldn't ignore the fact that he was running as someone was chasing him on an ATV.

Lao turned his head and saw three four-wheelers heading his way. A few members of the group were still running behind, not even close to catching up to him, but he knew he would not outrun the vehicles.

He looked around; he had nowhere to hide in the middle of a dirt field. He felt like a deer in hunting season, ready to be shot.

He took another step when something tugged on his foot. He let out an agonizing grunt as he looked back to see a root tripping him. He tried to stabilize himself, but it was no use. He was falling and falling fast.

His hands caught his body from falling hard onto the ground. His chin hit the soil and his lips tasted the brown dirt. A small cloud of dust rose, blurring his vision.

He kicked off the root and started crawling on all fours as if his life depended on it. The light of the four-wheelers blinded him as they surrounded him like a group of lions circling a wounded antelope.

"What do you want?" Lao screamed, raising his hands in surrender. He could hear someone getting off of their ATV, but he couldn't see the person. All he could see was the blinding light like an actor on a stage.

No one said anything.

Lao looked into the light as a stranger walked in front, breaking the beam from his eyes. He reached out his hand, "Come here, son," a man said with a gentle tone. "We're here to help you."

"Help?" Lao stood confused under the darkened sky among a group of strangers. He wondered what they could do to help.

"Come with us," the man said with a gentle voice. "I think we have some answers for you."

CHAPTER 29

Lao cautiously got on the back of a four-wheeler, wrapping his arms around the driver's waist as they returned to the barn on the rough soil at a much slower pace.

"Just listen to us," the older man pleaded as he parked the ATV. Two other four-wheelers joined them behind the barn as the group of walkers knocked on the barn door one at a time to enter.

"My name is Elijah," the older man greeted under the light of the moon as two others walked up beside him.

"I'm Enoch," another gentleman added as the lone woman walked up from her four-wheeler.

"I'm Judith," she welcomed and then headed toward the barn door.

"I'm..." Lao started before the group hushed him.

"It's not time for that," Elijah instructed as he patted Lao on his back. The three strangers headed toward the door. Judith and Enoch knocked and went in as Elijah stopped and looked over at the forest. He then looked over at Lao and nodded his head.

Lao looked over at the woods and saw the whistler standing by. "You see him too?"

Elijah didn't answer the question but gave Lao a warm smile. He knocked on the door six times and entered.

Lao walked over to the entrance of the barn door. He stopped and peeked through a slit in the wood panels and couldn't see anything. He opened the door, and it looked like a dark, empty hay barn.

"Huh?" Lao said confused as he walked into the middle of the barn. He looked around the barn with the pitchforks and shovels hanging on the walls. A rusted tractor sat under a hayloft, but he was confused. He saw at least a dozen people go in and now it was empty.

He looked around the emptiness.

He poked his head out of the barn and saw the whistler still standing at the entrance of the woods.

He stepped outside of the barn and closed the door. He opened it again and nothing happened.

He thought back to the video he had watched and remembered the knocking. He raised his hand, stared at his clenched fist, and slowly started.

Knock.

Knock.

Knock.

Knock.

Knock.

He stopped and looked behind him. He felt like the whistler was watching his every move.

It was.

Knock.

He gripped the handle and opened the door as it creaked from years of weather and wear. Poking in his head, he saw a group of strangers standing around in green robes. Lao stepped into the barn as a woman at the door grabbed his hand. She squeezed his hand comfortingly and led him to the group.

"Who comes before us now?" a voice asked from somewhere in the room.

Lao stood in the middle looking around the room full of robed strangers. He remembered Elijah telling him *"We're here to help,"* so he was going to give them a try.

"Lao," he weakly answered.

"We cannot hear you," the man said. "Louder!"

Lao looked around the room and weighed the pros and cons. But he still wanted to trust the old man.

"Lao!" he shouted.

As he yelled, the group joined in the roar.

CHAPTER 30

"Silence," the spokesman roared. A hush filled the room as someone gave Lao a green robe to put on over his clothing. "Lao, you probably have many questions. You may be wondering who we are. Why are you here? What is going on?" He stopped and lowered his hood as the entire group lowered theirs as well.

"My name is Enoch Welch," he proceeded as he bowed his head to the group and to Lao. "This group you are now part of is a group of people that does not discriminate based upon sex, race, age, money, or status. We are a group that does not choose our members, but our members choose us unknowingly. You, Lao, unknowingly became a member of our society, just as all of us did. It happened without our choice. It happened without our knowledge. It happened in an instant.

"You may be wondering what our group is called; throughout history we have been called many things. What you call yourself doesn't matter because our group itself doesn't have a name. We are who we are. No names needed.

"We do have a few rules, not created through by-laws or a vote, but created for us. They are rules we must follow. We may not want to, but we are required to adhere to them. If you don't, there are consequences. But it is interesting to know, we do not even know all the rules we are to abide by, but only know what we have tried through trial and error."

A woman stepped forward and took over the meeting. "Please listen to everything we are about to say; it is important to listen to every word. We are not allowed to repeat this introduction until a new member joins us. It could be tomorrow night. It could be next week. It could be a year. So, please listen." She stepped back and another man stepped forward on the other side of the circle.

"You may have noticed your tendencies that were normal a short time ago have shifted. You have probably experienced some differences in tiredness, exertion, hunger, and comfort just to name a few. And you will continue to experience them. Your hunger will not return. Your need for sleep has vanished. Your ability to never tire will be ongoing." Elijah stopped.

"Son," Elijah said compassionately. "I don't know how to tell you this, but that thing you have seen lately, you will always see from now on. It will follow you for the rest of your existence."

Lao's eyes went wide with dread.

"But that thing is the least of your worries because it cannot do anything to you, Lao. It cannot physically harm you." Elijah stepped forward and walked toward Lao. "Son, have you heard the adage if a tree falls in the middle of a forest and no one hears it, does it make a sound?"

Lao nodded his head.

"Good, then maybe knowing that will help with this next bit."

"Okay." Lao scanned the room of watching eyes, fixated on only him. He was hopeful but also unsure.

"Son, think back. Have you done something that should have hurt you but it didn't? Have you walked away from a car crash unscathed with just a gash on your head?" he asked pointing at the cut that hadn't healed. "Have you fallen from a tree and gotten up like nothing had happened? Have you experienced something that didn't seem possible? Now was anyone around you when these accidents happened?"

Lao looked around the room with doubt in his eyes.

"It's okay, Lao. You may not think you have experienced something like that, but you have." He took another step forward. "We all have experienced something like this. I had a heart attack while my wife was at the grocery store. And Judith had a freak diving accident in the shallow part of a pond. And Enoch had a hunting accident. Do you know what happened to you?"

Lao shook his head. "I don't know what you are talking about."

Enoch took over once again. "Lao, listen to me carefully. In the last day, when no one was around you," he stopped and looked at Judith and then back at Lao, "you died."

"What?" Lao blurted in shock. "I'm...I'm...I'm not dead."

"But you are, Lao," Judith said maternally. "You are, just like we all are."

"Am I, uh, a ghost?" Lao asked, remembering that he talked with his friends at school today like nothing had happened.

"No," Judith smiled warmly, "you are not a ghost."

"It doesn't matter how it happened," Enoch stepped in. "It may take some time to figure it out, but you will. We all have figured out how it happened to us. And knowing how it happened has given each of us some closure. But you will eventually see it."

"So, what's that thing I see now? Do you see it too?"

"Yes, we see it too," Elijah nodded. "That thing is your angel of death."

"But I thought you said that it can't hurt me," Lao rebutted. "If it's my angel of death, it's eventually going to get me!" he added with a surge of fear.

"No. No, it can't," Elijah said shaking his head. "The angel of death can't get you because you are already dead."

Lao looked at him in disbelief.

"You're an immortal," Enoch said as he continued to speak.

But just as the woman warned earlier in the night, Lao stopped listening after he heard the word *immortal*.

Enoch continued to talk as a smile appeared on Lao's face.

When Enoch finished his important speech, Elijah leaned over and whispered in his ear. "He quit listening when he heard that word, just like we thought he would."

CHAPTER 31

Lao returned home a little before 5 a.m. in order to grab his backpack for school and run out the door to make it in time for swim practice.

He remembered he would not get tired, so instead of walking to school like he normally would, he ran. He didn't just jog, but sprinted. He arrived at the locker room without feeling tired or out of breath.

He quickly undressed and put on his swimming briefs and headed for the pool. No one was there yet, so he got a few laps in.

He felt invincible. He understood why he was so powerful yesterday morning when he beat Reid in all their races. He was ready to see Reid's cocky smile droop when he beat him again today.

"Lao!" Coach Haman shouted causing him to get out of the pool. Haman gave out partners for warm-ups and teamed Reid with Lao.

"Lao," Reid mumbled as he hung up his towel.

"Morning, Reid," Lao returned as they followed the rest of the team to dive into the pool.

They did a few warm-up laps as Reid trash-talked Lao every time they met in the middle.

"Did you shoot up this morning?" Reid asked as he kicked water in Lao's face.

"You'll need it to beat me." Lao swam away briskly without losing his cool or breath. "Go ahead and try."

Coach Haman blew his whistle and everyone started to get out of the pool. Lao felt a chill in the air and a growing whistle in his ears. He pulled himself out of the water and turned around to see the angel of death standing near the pool. For the first time, he wasn't afraid of the creature. He just ignored him.

The overhead lights flickered as a few swimmers were still in the pool. Jessica looked up and saw one of the long fluorescent light bulbs spark. The long line of light bulbs overhead swayed as if coming undone.

"Get out of the pool!" Haman screamed as he saw a few of the swimmers still trying to reach the edge.

Lao looked around the pool and found the darkness had spread in the water like blood. It ebbed closer to Jessica who was still ten feet away from the edge.

"Come on!" Reid screamed to Jessica as he heard a loud pop as sparks flew overhead like a sparkler. One last pop echoed in everyone's ears.

Snap!

Screams commingled with the whistle in the air as a long line of bright lights, still connected to one another fell from the ceiling leaving one stuck to the electrical power outlet.

"Jessica!" Haman screamed as he watched in fear.

The falling lights flickered like strobe lights at a dance party as the electrical current hit the pool's water. Jessica screamed in agony and then fell beneath the waves.

Lao watched wide-eyed in shock. He watched Jessica's body sink further to the bottom of the water until it vanished into the blackness. He kept watch. He couldn't turn his head or close his eyes. It was as if he was being forced to watch her death.

Suddenly, the dark water cleared. He could see Jessica's hair moving with the tides, but nothing else. The angel of death surfaced in the water, rising dry with no sign of having been in water with its robe flowing effortlessly.

Lao couldn't take his eyes off of it even though the rest of the people huddled around Jessica's lifeless body. Suddenly, the angel of death left the area. The frigidness was gone and so was the whistle.

"Call for help!" someone screamed as Lao woke up to their fearful screams. "Jessica!"

Reid reached his hand to touch to the water to see if it was safe, but Coach Haman grabbed his wrist. "Reid! No!"

Lao stood by confused by what had just happened.

Why did my angel of death take her?

CHAPTER 32

They canceled school for the day to allow students to grieve the loss of Jessica, but most of the people just saw it as a day off and wished they had been told before making it to school.

"Want to go to Pop's for breakfast?" Smyrna asked as the four friends stood in the school parking lot.

"Sounds good to me," Phil said as Thya nodded her head.

"Sounds like we are going to Pop's," Lao confirmed as Thya hooked her elbow with his.

"How are you doing?" she asked.

"I'm okay." Lao shrugged his shoulders.

"What happened?" Phil asked. "I heard some things, but you were actually there."

"It was a freak accident. One minute we were swimming laps and then the next, the lights fell and it electrocuted her."

"Tragic," Smyrna gasped as she clung to Phil's hand.

"Yeah," Lao said.

"Poor Reid," Thya said to the group.

"Reid?" Lao asked shocked. "They were together?"

"Hot and heavy, I was told," Smyrna commented as they journeyed downtown to the oldest eating establishment of Sardis.

"He'll be fine," Lao said aloof. "Pretty boy Reid will find a new girl tomorrow."

"Jealous much?" Phil said with a haughty tone.

"No."

"Then what?" Thya asked.

"You don't hear what he says in the locker room," he fictitiously alluded. Even though he used to date Thya, Lao didn't have a problem with Reid until yesterday when he started questioning his swimming abilities.

"To be a fly on that wall, a hot steamy locker room with a bunch of naked ripped guys," Smyrna said with a twisted smile as Phil gave her a gaping look. "Whatever, don't look at me like that. You would do anything to see the cheerleaders changing."

Phil didn't deny her claim and just shrugged his shoulders.

They walked into Pop's, which was a country-style restaurant with farm utensils and equipment used as décor. The four of them walked to the hostess stand who quickly seated them beside a wall of sharp hoes, hard shovels, pointy rakes, and polished trowels.

The waitress took their drink orders and left them with the menus to look over.

"I always love this place," Smyrna said as she looked around at the antique gardening equipment dangling overhead. "It's like a treat for your taste buds and eyes."

"You're so weird," Thya laughed as she looked down at the menu, deciding between waffles or French toast.

"Whatever. It's also cute to see the old men sitting around drinking coffee," Smyrna said waving at a group of gray-headed men sipping their morning beverage a few tables away. "Adorable."

Lao looked over, and one man gave him a wink.

Elijah?

CHAPTER 33

The four friends spent the day together until it was evening, and Lao and Thya split off to celebrate their six-month anniversary at Frost's, a 1950s-themed ice cream parlor near the center of town, a block away from Central Park.

"I'll take a hot fudge sundae with nuts, whipped cream, and two cherries to go," Lao ordered to Walter, a good looking sandy-blond guy who appeared to be a recent high school graduate.

"That sounds tasty," Thya gushed. "I'll take the same."

"The same?" Lao laughed out loud. "When did you start liking nuts and cherries?"

"Oh, I mean without the nuts and cherries," she quickly corrected. "I was just thinking of the hot fudge since it's getting chilly outside."

"I thought you always got a banana milkshake with fresh strawberries added on top," he said playfully, handing Walter a ten at the cash register that chimed like it did in 1952.

"A girl has a right to choose something different, doesn't she?" she said with her hand on her hip and a smile on her face.

"Just wanted you to know I know what you like," he said taking his change from Walter.

Lao saw the lights dim and a chill come into the store. He looked at the door, but no one came in. He turned his head around and saw the whistler standing beside Walter chopping the nuts with a sharp blue paring knife.

"Be careful, Walter," Lao cautioned as the whistler acknowledged the remark. He raised up his robed arm and lifted his skeleton-like hands and waved a single finger as if condemning Lao's last remark.

Lao heard a light whistle as the red circle on his face intensified its glow.

Walter swept up the nuts and sprinkled them on top of one sundae with the knife still in his right hand. He spun around looking for a jar of cherries when his foot got caught on the plastic floor mat behind the counter.

He yelped out as he started to fall, holding the paring knife in his hand.

"Walter! Drop the knife!" Lao shouted as the whistler blew a deafening blow, causing all the circles on his face to burn a bright red.

Lao jumped over the counter and found Walter lying on his stomach without a knife in sight.

"Walter!" Lao belted bending down.

Walter rolled over laughing. "I'm such a klutz," he hollered with a wink as Lao helped him to his feet.

Lao grabbed the two sundaes and turned to see the whistler still standing beside the oblivious Walter. Lao and Thya waved goodbye and headed to Central Park with their sundaes. He didn't feel right about leaving the angel of death back there, but he didn't want to be around it anymore either.

They proceeded to the park and sat on a bench under an oak tree. Even though they had spent the entire day together, they still had things to say.

"Promise me we will always be like this," Lao urged.

"Like what?" Thya asked, taking a spoonful of hot fudge.

"Like this" Lao pointed out sticking his spoon back in his sundae, turning to Thya to give her a sweet kiss.

"I promise," she agreed as their lips parted.

They sat on the park bench and watched people walking home as they were closing up their local boutiques of women's hats and house décor. They saw a few young couples running by in their jogging tights and some older couples walking their dogs.

Lao took another bite of his sundae, forcing himself to eat it, as a chill surrounded him.

He looked around as Thya continued to eat her sundae without feeling the drop of temperature.

"What's wrong?" she asked as she looked over and noticed Lao's watchful eyes darting around the scene.

"I...I don't know," he answered suspiciously. "I just felt like something was wrong."

"You need to calm down," she said, leaning into his shoulder. "I think Jessica's death rattled you today."

"Yeah, maybe," he thought. But there was another reason. He saw the angel of death leaning down behind them as if observing the ice cream Thya was eating. He continued to lean further down until his head was directly between the two.

Lao fixed his eyes on the window display across the street, hoping the whistler would leave.

Thya patted his leg as she turned to look at him, looking through the whistler. Lao turned, but all he could see was the whistler's mask three inches from his nose. He gulped; his hands frozen as he heard a soft whistle.

He closed his eyes and opened them. The whistler was gone.

But the whistling remained.

"Help!" a woman screamed from behind them.

Lao jumped up and started running in the scream's direction. He ran through the park and saw a distant woman behind the white grand gazebo kneeling down. "Help!"

Lao came up running and saw an older man lying in the grass clutching his heart.

"Do something!" the woman screamed to the two teenagers as Thya pulled out her phone and dialed for emergency. Lao tried to bend down to start CPR, but he couldn't move. He froze once again. He couldn't turn his head. He couldn't speak. He couldn't even blink.

The angel of death forced him to watch as it bent down and touched the shivering man on his head. Suddenly, he stopped moving, and Lao knew the man was dead.

The angel had left. The darkness had vanished. The whistling had subsided. He was once again able to move freely and started administering CPR even though he knew the chest compressions were useless.

But he wanted to keep up appearances for Thya.

CHAPTER 34

Lao stood in his bedroom staring at his alarm clock that signaled 1:24 a.m. He stood guard, seeing the shadow was once again in the corner, as if it was its permanent resting spot.

His mind churned with questions. The more he lingered in that thought process, the more overwhelmed he became from the loss of solid answers.

He turned on his television and flipped through the channels hoping to find the one from last night showing the meeting place. He scanned through the channels six times and never came across a night vision, time-stamped show.

He clicked the television off and stood in thought. He considered exercising, but wondered if it did him any good since he was immortal. Another question he wanted to ask.

The night lingered like stale air.

He saw the millions of promising opportunities of being an immortal, but he was seeing a few drawbacks. Only a few. He hoped that with answers, the drawbacks would become minimal.

The alarm clock flipped to the next hour as curiosity got the better of him.

Maybe there's a meeting every night.

He grabbed his keys and tiptoed down the hall. He didn't leave a note for his mother this time since he knew he would be back. He couldn't die in a car crash or anything, so there was no use in leaving a note.

He drove through the deserted town hitting all five green lights before turning off onto the country road in silence. He didn't feel like listening to music, having learned to enjoy the silence when the whistler wasn't causing his ears to bleed. Silence was now a welcomed friend, a roommate he never wanted to kick out.

He turned onto the state route and slowed as he saw the tree he'd parked in front of the night before. But this time there was another vehicle parked there. A navy Chevrolet Silverado with a back window decal of 13.1, signaling completion of a half-marathon.

Lao parked his mother's car and journeyed to the barn. He wondered if someone new was coming tonight.

Maybe he'd get more answers.

This time he would listen more closely.

CHAPTER 35

Lao exited the forest and noticed a man hobbling toward the barn. His right leg was twisted inward and his left leg appeared a few inches shorter, causing an exaggerated limp. His back twisted like a curlicue as his neck tilted sideways. Lao watched the uncomfortable looking man, feeling compassion for him.

The man reached the barn door and stood on the outside. He opened the door and peeped his head in and then closed it, confused.

Lao walked up startling him from behind. He quickly turned as the moonlight shone his uneven cheekbones and flattened nose on the disfigured man's face. His face had unhealed scratch marks and cuts scattered all over.

"I'm sorry to frighten you. Are you here for the meeting?"

The man looked at Lao puzzled, scanning him from top to bottom. He opened his mouth, but slurred speech came out as he tried to connect his undistinguishable words.

"Yeah, da neeting here?"

Lao nodded his head and winked at the injured man. He raised up his hand and knocked on the barn door six times, causing the room behind the door to become alive.

The man tried to follow Lao, but the woman at the door stopped him.

"No," she said calmly and closed it.

"Why did you do that?" Lao asked.

The woman handed Lao his green robe. "It's the rule. You have to come in alone."

Lao walked into the room as a few of the other immortals greeted him. They seemed to know his name, but he only knew of three of theirs—Elijah, Enoch, and Judith.

Lao found Elijah and whispered in his ear. "I have questions."

"I know, son," Elijah nodded sympathetically, "but the questions will have to wait until a new member arrives."

"But..." Lao started before Elijah shook his head.

"It's the rule," he explained solemnly. "We warned you to listen. But our lips our bound to the rules. You understand, son?"

Lao nodded his head as he let out a huff.

Elijah's eyes widened with hope as the disfigured man came through the door. "Looks like it's your lucky night."

CHAPTER 36

The meeting started the same way it had the night before.

"Who comes before us now?"

The man spoke feebly, but it was unrecognizable.

"Will you please repeat that and say it louder?" the speaker commanded.

"Br—ch!" the man sputtered with trembling lips.

"I am sorry, but can you say it again?"

"Br-a-n-ch!" the man yelled from the left corner of his mouth.

Various members stepped forward in their circle and started giving the new guest an overview.

A woman stepped forward to recite the script she was given "Please listen to everything we are about to say. You may stop listening, but it is important to listen to every word. We are not allowed to repeat this introduction until a new member joins us. It could be tomorrow night. It could be next week. It could be a year. So, please listen."

Lao stood to attention. He wanted to pull out his phone and record the next bit in case he missed anything, but subconsciously he knew it would not be allowed.

Elijah stepped forward. "Do you know how you died?"

Branch tried his best to spit out a sentence as concise as he could. Everyone looked around unable to understand everything, but they each knew what happened. A car had hit him the other night.

"Good, Branch," Elijah nodded. "Knowing how you died will help you along the process."

"Do you know where it happened?" Judith stepped forward and asked.

He nodded his head on his crooked neck as he pointed forward.

"It was on this road?" Judith asked as Branch nodded once again.

"When did this happen? Do you remember?" Judith asked again.

"Hal-o-een," he stuttered as Lao watched intently.

"We are here to help you on this journey," Judith concluded as she stepped back.

"As we have said, you are immortal. You will not experience death. There are both positives and negatives with this existence. You will not experience any pain or discomfort. You will never tire or grow hungry. You will not age or decay," Elijah said with no emotion.

"But I am sorry to say," he started as a look of consolation landed on his face, "though you will not get any worse in your appearance, you will also not get any better."

"So, you mean…" Branch started as Enoch interrupted him.

"Yes, we mean you will never be back to your old self. You will be in the state you are in for the rest of time. Though you are not in any pain, you will never be able to stand up straight. Though you can walk, you will always have that debilitating limp. The wounds on your face and body will never heal. Your speech will never improve. The way you look today will be how you look in a thousand years."

"No!" Branch erupted in a flood of tears. "It's not my alt. It's not my alt I got 'it by car."

"I know, Branch," Enoch consoled. "We all know that it's not your fault you got hit by a car, but there is nothing we can do. You have to learn to live with it."

"I'd ather die," he croaked out between sobs.

"But you can't die," Enoch emphasized. "You're immortal."

Branch looked up devastated as if his worst fear had come true.

Lao's face also dropped when a memory from Halloween night floated into his mind.

CHAPTER 37

Lao's mind went back to being in the backseat of Phil's car driving down this same road. He remembered the taste of Thya's lip gloss and how the cinnamon made his lips tingle. Or it may have been her lips, themselves, causing the stir.

He remembered Thya falling into his lap as Phil swerved.

He'd said something about a truck being on the side of the road. A truck with a flat tire on the backside.

A few seconds later Smyrna yelled there was a deer. Or she thought it was a deer.

Phil and Lao got out of the car and examined the damage. There was no dark fur on the bumper. There was nothing that would signal a deer, even though the dent was massive on the front end.

Lao retraced the memory as he caught an important detail he'd originally overlooked.

There was a large, deep scratch on the side of the car near the front bumper. A scratch that was overlooked because the dent stole their attention.

But would a deer cause a scratch, Lao wondered.

No, but a belt buckle could.

He remembered walking to the car and hearing heavy breathing. The sound of death approaching.

But it wasn't a deer.

It was Branch. Dying alone. Becoming immortal.

CHAPTER 38

Lao returned his focus to the meeting. He hoped he hadn't zoned out too much and missed any more important details, but it seemed he was only out for a flash.

"I'm sorry, Branch, truly," Enoch said as he stepped back.

Someone new stepped forward and started again. "The angel of death that we mentioned earlier will still follow you. But he isn't following to get you." The woman stopped, making sure everyone in the room was listening. "He's following to get revenge."

"Revenge?" Lao gasped.

The woman looked over at Lao and nodded her head. "Since we all have evaded death by dying when no one was around to witness it, we have somehow fallen into a loophole, per se, where the angel of death has no power. And this has caused it to be filled with animosity.

"Since the angel of death cannot take you, it will take everyone else around you." She stopped and looked Lao in the eyes. "As some of you have already noticed, no one around you is safe."

"Is there something we can do?" Lao erupted before quickly covering his mouth for interrupting rudely.

"It's okay, Lao," the woman said as she stopped and looked around the room. "This is the only time we can talk freely and ask questions, during the introduction meeting for a new member. We may not answer everything because we still do not know the full answer to some questions."

Enoch stepped forward and the woman stepped back. "To answer your question, Lao, there is nothing we can do."

"Nothing?" Lao replied in shock. "Can't we tell people to not come around us?"

"No. If you try, your mouth will suddenly become stilled and anyone around you will immediately die."

"Immediately," Elijah stressed shaking his head. Lao saw the look of remorse on his face. It was a look that signaled he had made this mistake already.

Enoch patted Elijah on his back and took over. "You may have already noticed this, but once the angel of death claims a victim, you will be bound to watch until the moment of death. You will not be able to turn your head or close your eyes. But as long as you can see them, they will die. This is how he exacts revenge. Being helpless is the worst feeling when a crisis is happening before your eyes."

"It's the feeling of helplessness that gives him strength and satisfaction," Judith said. "And it seems the more you give in to that feeling, the more he takes.

"This is crucial, but it's also the hardest part. If you can learn to be unfazed during his kills, he will not kill your loved ones as much. But once he finds your sweet spot, he will continue to go after them until it's gone," she said.

"So, after all my friends and family are gone, the angel will leave?" Lao looked down with a downcast expression.

Enoch stepped forward and shook his head. "That's not how it works. You are immortal. Even if you become a hermit and cut yourself off from existence, the angel of death will find ways to bring people into your life."

Lao looked around the crowd of people who had been dealing with this for years. "Does it get easier?"

Each member turned to their neighbor in the circle, as if consulting one another.

"I'm not sure *easier* is a good word," a man suggested as he stepped forward and removed his robe's hood and gave Lao a wink.

"Walter?"

CHAPTER 39

The meeting concluded answering many of Lao's questions. He didn't feel great with the newfound knowledge, but he still felt like understanding was a powerful tool. But knowing the truth about Branch was almost too much to bear.

"So, you figured it out?" Walter asked as groups huddled around the barn.

"Figured what out?" Lao asked defensively.

"You know, how you died," Walter said nonchalantly like he was asking about the hot fudge sundae.

"Oh," Lao said relieved, thinking maybe Walter knew the truth about him and Branch. "The only thing I can think of is when I fell in the cemetery the other night, I must have hit my head and died."

"In a cemetery? Oh, what a way to go. To be so close to death and not taste it. Bummer."

"So, you wish you had died normally?"

"Well," Walter said in an apprehensive voice, "I've gotten used to this. But the first few decades were a hard adjustment."

Lao looked at him in confusion. "Decades?"

"How old do you think I am?" he asked with a playful smile.

"I was thinking eighteen," Lao answered.

"I was nineteen when I died. In 1777."

"You mean, you are--"

"Lao, we are immortals," he said wide-eyed. "I'm a baby in this room compared to some people in here."

"Don't people realize that you aren't aging? How do you hide that?"

"Sometimes you have to move from place to place and start over," he elaborated shrugging his shoulders. "But the human race is selfish. They focus more on themselves than others."

"But don't people start to wonder why you still look nineteen when they look fifty?"

"You've heard the expression 'good genes'?" he smiled wickedly. "Yeah, there is no such thing as good genes, but people don't believe in immortals, so that's the only logical explanation."

Lao continued to listen to Walter talk as he discussed how he lived with being immortal. After ten minutes, Branch limped away from a circle and headed toward the door.

"One second," Lao said as he ran up to Branch. "I'm sorry, Branch," he sympathized as the disfigured man nodded his head. "I just found out last night, myself."

"Ooks like ou died a nice deaf," he stumbled over the words.

Guilt rushed over Lao as he understood clearly what Branch meant. *Looks like you died a nice death.*

"Ooks like my unnin days are gone."

Lao nodded his head, feeling sadness that the man's joy of running was a distant memory. No more marathons for him. He'd be lucky to walk a mile without stares.

"I wish I knew what to say." Lao stood nearby and watched Branch with his twisted arm open the swinging barn door. He wanted to run over and help him, but at the same time, he wanted to never let him in again.

"It's okay, I gonna ind da car dat hit me an get da angel ta gill him. I ramember what 'it me."

Those words haunted Lao's ears as Walter walked up and patted him on the back as they both watched the hobbling man limp away. *It's okay, I'm gonna find the car that hit me and get the angel to kill him. I remember what hit me.*

"Poor bloke," Walter said shaking his head. "I would hate to spend eternity looking like that," he stopped. "Women say they can look past looks, but they won't look past that. Ain't that right, stud?" Walter patted Lao's flat stomach like an old friend.

Lao nodded his head. He hadn't even thought of that part of immortality.

"You can sleep around as much as you want, Lao. You won't have any kids since you don't have any DNA to lose anymore. You can't contract any diseases. It's like a bachelor's paradise," he winked. "Enjoy it while you can," he laughed. "That's right, you will always enjoy it, swimming man. Ladies go nuts for athletes," Walter said as he felt Lao's biceps through his bulky sweatshirt. "Just don't intrude on my reach," he smiled. "Deal?"

"Deal," Lao agreed with a fake smile.

"One other thing. Never, ever, go into the farmhouse."

"Why?" Lao asked confused.

"Just believe me," he said. "But it's your life."

Walter walked away, scoping out his next target for a possible one-night stand amid immortals as Lao stood at the door.

He didn't know what he could do to warn his friends. But it seemed like their fate was sealed. Death was coming from either his angel of death or Branch's.

CHAPTER 40

Lao was on edge at school all day. He felt at any minute he was going to witness a sabotage by the angel of death to kill another one of his acquaintances or friends. He breathed a sigh of relief once his closest friends departed school and he loaded up on a school bus with the rest of his swim team to the meet in the neighboring town.

The guys sat around in silence in their swim briefs in the locker room, looking at one another, not as teammates but as competition. This wasn't just another swim meet, but district finals that would allow the two fastest swimmers to proceed to regionals and then to state.

"How are you doing, Reid?" Samuel finally asked, breaking the tension or possibly playing mind games.

"I'm swimming in Jessica's memory today," Reid announced solemnly, sitting on the bench with his elbows on his knees, resting his head on his hands.

"Good luck," Samuel commented as the rest of the team echoed him unconvincingly.

Coach Haman walked into the locker room, eyeing his team judgmentally. "Reid, Lao, Trent, you're up."

Lao exited the locker room looking in the stands to see a crowd of unfamiliar faces. He smiled at the relief of not knowing anyone in the stands.

They announced the eight swimmers as the crowd clapped and roared while Lao's heart dropped like a belly flop into the water. Thya walked into the pool arena with her little sister who had a sucker in her mouth, followed by the angel of death.

Lao wanted to shout for Thya to watch out, but his throat went silent as he waved ferociously for their attention. Thya waved and blew him a kiss as she clutched onto her little sister's tiny hand and walked up the bleachers.

The angel of death sat behind little Abby, watching her lick her pink lollipop as if he wanted to taste the sweetness.

"Take your position!" the announcer commanded as the eight racers got on their starting blocks.

Lao bent his knees and braced himself for the race, but he focused his attention somewhere else. He lifted his head to watch Abby and hoped the angel was just toying with him.

The announcer hit the button for the countdown, and three seconds later eight boys jumped into the water to swim the two-hundred meter freestyle.

Lao took an early lead but with every stroke, he watched Abby from the water. He wanted to close his eyes, but he couldn't. He didn't want to shatter Thya's world, even if she would never know Abby's death was because of him.

He reached the fifty meters mark and executed an exquisite tumble turn. He glided under the water with his strong dolphin kick, leaving Reid a full body length behind.

He popped his head up to the surface and looked over at Abby as he could finally focus entirely on the race.

The angel of death had left.

Abby was safe.

CHAPTER 41

Lao swam like a fish, streaking through the water with his powerful, kicking legs and strong, toned arms. He reached the halfway mark as he heard Coach Haman screaming his name to keep swimming.

Lao was the happiest he had ever been. The crowd was watching in awe at his speed and tenacity. His coach was cheering him on to reach another school record. He glanced over at Thya who was jumping up and down, full of enthusiasm. He scanned his competitors, and none of them were close.

He reached the other end of the pool and completed his last tumble turn and exploded off the wall as if it shot him out of a cannon. He reached the halfway mark in the pool and knew he would easily head to regionals. There was no way anyone was going catch him now.

Especially with his newfound ability of not tiring.

He was ten strokes away from the wall and kept his face down in the water for the last stretch. He looked below and saw a blackness swirling underneath the next lane.

A frigidness hit him, causing his body to convulse. He didn't want to look at the next lane, but his head was turning beyond his control.

"No!" he screamed under the water as he felt his momentum drain. He held out his hand and drifted to the wall, but his flow suddenly stopped as if someone was pulling his leg in the other direction.

His eyes widened as he saw Reid fighting the angel of death like a life-or-death game of water polo.

"Hel-" Reid gargled as he was being held under by the villainous beast, as if being baptized into his death.

Lao wanted to swim to his rescue, but he couldn't move his arms or legs. He was floating like a dead man on his stomach in Reid's direction. He tried to scream for help, but his mouth only filled with chlorinated water. He swallowed the bitterness and tried to scream again, but his mouth filled once again with pool water.

Reid was tossing and turning, sinking under water like someone caught him in a fisherman's net dragging him below the surface. His mouth opened as silent screams and air bubbles escaped while his body tensed as his muscles rippled. His tired legs were kicking, but the race had exhausted him.

Lao kept his eyes fixed on the deadly scene. His eyes connected with Reid's. Reid looked at him with confusion and fear. He looked at him in need of a rescue. He looked at him like he was being betrayed.

Reid let out one final scream. No one heard it, but Lao read his lips. Just one last word.

Reid's eyes glazed over as the life force within him gave up. His sandy blond hair floated hauntingly still. Just a moment ago, he was fighting for his life, and now he was sinking in his death.

Lao's body unfroze as the angel of death vanished. He swam to the boy who had been his good friend until just two days ago. They had been like brothers, but the last word Reid said was going to haunt Lao for many days to come. He dove under the water and grabbed hold of Reid's firm arms.

The crowd was screaming in horror as Lao brought up the bluing body, pulling him to the pool's edge.

Coach Haman started CPR, but Lao knew it would not do any good.

The angel of death had done its deed.

It had another act of revenge under its belt.

Lao stood by watching and waiting with his teammates who were bowing their heads in prayer. Lao knew it was useless, but he didn't want to be the lone man out. He bowed his head and closed his eyes.

Be strong! Lao told himself as he remembered the instructions to appear jaded at the time of death so the angel wouldn't get any pleasure out of looking at his sorrow. But Lao couldn't control his emotions.

An image of Reid's last word hit him, causing his knees to quake. Lao looked into Reid's placid eyes and wondered what he meant. Was he asking about Lao's sudden swimming phenomenon or about his own death? But deep-down Lao knew the meaning behind the lone word.

Why?

CHAPTER 42

The EMTs arrived and rushed Reid's dead body to the hospital, doing their best to find a glimmer of hope in a bleak situation. Lao watched as one of the first responders shook her head to another before exiting the swim arena.

"What happened?" Thya asked as Lao appeared from the locker room in his blue jeans and sweatshirt after they cancelled the swim meet.

"He died," Lao answered solemnly, smiling kindly to Abby who was playing on Thya's phone.

"No, what happened with you?" she prodded, lowering her voice so the last remaining students and parents didn't overhear their conversation.

"What do you mean?" he asked, scrunching his face in confusion.

"You…" She stopped and looked around to make sure it was safe to say. "You froze in the water."

Lao's eyes widened as he suddenly knew what a caught rabbit felt like in a snare trap.

"I, uh," he stammered, looking down at his three-month-old sneakers that were marked up from high school shenanigans.

"Why didn't you try to save him?" she asked softly. "You didn't even try." She closed her watering eyes as a lone tear fell. Looking away from Lao she tugged her little sister's hand. "Come on, Abby."

"Thya! Wait," Lao croaked. He watched the two walk away, but he had to stop them. He had to try. He jogged up to her and grabbed her arm. "You have to listen to me."

"*Why?*" She folded her arms as a tear slid down her cheek.

That question stung Lao's heart as it was the same question Reid asked before he died.

"You were talking bad about him two days ago. And now," she stopped and looked at the pool over Lao's shoulder, "now he's dead."

"I couldn't save him," Lao said as he watched a sliver of a shadow slide under the door, oozing closer like overflowing water spilling over the rim of a cup.

"We saw you," Thya scolded with her voice rising in uncertainty. "We saw you stop swimming and float toward him. But you stopped swimming toward him too. You just looked like someone watching him in the water."

Lao listened to her words. He'd wanted to rescue Reid. He'd wanted to swim and help his friend, even though their relationship had taken a bad turn. He'd wanted to save him, but it forced his body to stop. He looked into her eyes and wanted to say everything he was thinking and feeling but knew he couldn't. He knew the removal of his guilt would just cause more heartache and pain for him. He had to watch his words and actions and try to keep the scales of his new life balanced somehow.

"I went into shock," Lao lied.

"Shock?" she spouted in disbelief. "Shock?"

"Yes, shock," he continued with the tale. "I couldn't believe my eyes. I think I even blacked out for a few seconds, because when I finally came to, he was already…" his voice quivered. He looked over and saw the shadow expanding.

He was showing sadness. The shadow was growing as if it was eating up the energy.

Lao refocused his attention. He had to find the mixture of jadedness and false sympathy. He needed to reel Thya back into his arms and also distance himself from her to save her.

"He was already dead," he insisted flatly. "There wasn't anything I could do."

Thya looked at him, eyeing him suspiciously. "There's something you're not telling me," she refuted as she skewed her eyes at him.

He nodded his head. "Some things are best unsaid."

"No," she replied looking into his eyes. "It's something else." She paused. "I warned you if you lie to me, it's over." She stopped and looked down at her sister and brushed her hair. "I wasn't lying."

Lao stood silent. He didn't know what to say because he realized no matter what he said, he would lose her, either with a lie. Or her death.

CHAPTER 43

Lao put on his green robe as a few of the fellow members he hadn't met before introduced themselves. He listened to their stories: a man who died in a freak accident in the Civil War, a woman who caught the black plague in modern-day Romania, and a friend of Julius Caesar's who died from a minor infection. Lao looked around the room and felt awed to be in the presence of people throughout pivotal moments of history.

He wanted to mingle around the group and listen to each of them regale in moments of heroic events. But it seemed no matter how much they spoke of the joyous aspects of being an immortal, they each walked the fine line of not speaking of the ill effects of their blessed curse.

"So, it seems like you are all glad you are immortal," Lao suggested, trying to dig into the darker aspects of their lives. He was already feeling the ramifications of the angel's revenge. He wanted to feel he wasn't alone.

Judith changed the topic when someone walked into the conversation. "Edgar, how are you?" she asked as the entire group refocused on Edgar, dismissing Lao's question.

He stood fixated at the swiftness of the change. He noticed it wasn't like a gradual cool autumn breeze, but a sudden tornado.

"I'm sorry," Lao said, interrupting their new conversation. "But is there something you don't want to share? Did I strike a nerve?"

Elijah took Lao by the arm and walked him away from the group like a caring grandfather. "Lao, we don't speak much of our tragedies when we are in the barn."

"But you warned me last night," Lao corrected.

"That was a customary introduction for new members. A meeting to help the new immortals on their upcoming journeys."

"But why not talk about it?" Lao harped. "Don't you want to get it out of your systems?"

Elijah shook his head. "Son, some people in this room have been getting it out of their system for a thousand years." He stopped and looked around his group of intertwined friends, "Now they want to pretend like they are normal."

"Normal?" Lao pursed his lips in thought at the strangeness of that phrase.

"Look around this barn, son. What does everyone have in common in here?" Elijah asked, showcasing the guests scattered among the bales of hay.

"They are all immortals," Lao answered, unsure of why that mattered.

"Exactly." Elijah's eyes lit up with a beaming smile. "What else do you see?"

Lao looked around but couldn't see a commonality. The group was broad. Once he thought he found a common thread, diversity's scissors would cut it.

"Maybe a better question is what do you *not* see?" Elijah winked.

Lao scanned the setting and found many things he didn't see, but the lack of an airplane pilot or someone fluent in Swahili didn't seem important.

"Do you see the shadow in here? Do you see anyone's angel of death?"

Lao shook his head.

"Exactly," Elijah grinned. "The angel of death cannot come into this barn because there would be no purpose for him being here. There isn't anyone he can take. We are all immortals." He stopped and patted Lao on his shoulder. "This is a safe place for people to come and know they will not have to see anyone die while they are here. So, if people don't like to talk about their tragedies, it isn't because they don't have any. It's just they have too many to count, and when they stand here," he stopped, looked around his band of brothers and sisters, "they are free." He smiled with a warm wink of acknowledgement.

Lao nodded his head and smiled. He understood the need for a safe place.

This may be a safe place for them, Lao thought as the barn door opened and Branch walked in, *but it's not for me.* Lao watched with empathy as the man limped in, trying his best to carry on a conversation as the woman at the door helped him with his robe. Lao looked at Branch who stared in his direction, walking toward him as his legs looked like twisted tree limbs after a hurricane.

"Do ou know da Ardohls?"

"Arnolds?" Lao replied, pretending to take a moment to think over the name. "I, uh," he stopped and looked around the room. "I can't say that I do," he lied. "Why?"

"I found da car dat 'it me," he said the best he could. "It uz a Ardohl."

Lao's eyes widened. He didn't expect to be having this conversation, especially this fast.

"Are you sure an Arnold was the one that hit you? Are you sure?"

Branch couldn't move his body very well, as if he was fighting with someone else controlling his limbs, but his wink was flawless.

"I know it uz da Ardolhs." He grabbed Lao's shoulder, pulling it down to whisper something into his ear.

Lao's eyes shot open as he understood Branch's broken words with no need for interpretation. He felt the balances on his scale shift. He understood why the group wanted to make this place a safe one. Because he needed a sanctuary right now.

"I saw the car that hit me in Butch's garage today. I asked him when the dented car came in and who the owner of it was." He stopped and let the words linger in Lao's ear. "He said Mr. Arnold dropped it off two days ago after his son hit a deer on State Route 118."

Branch let go of his shoulder, but Lao didn't quickly straighten his back. He was off kilter himself with the haunting words.

"You know," Branch enunciated with perfect clarity, "I was that deer."

CHAPTER 44

Lao got to school early, sitting in the cafeteria waiting for his friends to show up. He tried to catch up on his reading assignment of Dante's *Inferno,* but he couldn't get past the writing style of the classic. Of course, the lurking shadow across the room didn't help things either.

Thya and Smyrna showed up with four doughnuts and lattes.

"Here you go," Smyrna said, while Thya seemed distant. She hadn't responded to Lao's text the previous night.

"I'm not hungry," Lao said as he folded a page and closed his paperback. "You can split it."

"Split it," Smyrna laughed. "Please." She picked up her donut and took a bite out of her chocolate cream filled. She giggled as the sides squirted out some sugary cream.

"How are you doing, Thya?" Lao asked. She shrugged her shoulders, looking through her purse for something.

"What's up with you two?" Smyrna asked, feeling the tension in the air. "Just kiss and make up."

"Where's Phil?" Thya asked, ignoring the question without even looking at Lao across the table.

"I don't know," Lao answered. "I haven't seen him."

"He texted me this morning saying he was going to get here early to study for his Latin test," Smyrna said. "He said he was going to meet us here."

"I haven't seen him all morning and I got here early myself," Lao added as a surge of fear hit him. "When did you last hear from him?"

They both looked at their phones.

"I got a text about an hour ago saying he was walking to school," Smyrna explained, confused by his question.

"Same," Thya commented flatly.

"Have you texted him lately?" Lao asked throwing his books in his backpack.

"Yeah, I asked what he wanted from the bakery, but he didn't answer," Smyrna said as she noticed the look on Lao's face. "What's wrong, Lao?"

"It's probably nothing," he lied as he asked them to go to the library to see if Phil was studying in there or in his Latin classroom. "Phil mentioned something to me yesterday, so I'm going to check on that," he lied again.

"Mentioned what?" Thya asked, but Lao had already walked away.

Lao ran through the school's hallways and pushed open the exit door. He started running to the first place he could think of, Pop's.

CHAPTER 45

"I'm sorry to interrupt," Lao said as he stood in front of a table of old men sipping their black coffee with newspapers in their hands.

"Lao!" Elijah said shocked. "What are you doing here?"

"Can I talk to you real quick?" he asked, standing nervously, knowing every minute mattered.

Elijah got up from the table and the two moved away from ear shot. "What is it, son?"

"Do you know much about Branch?"

"Son, we shouldn't be doing this out here," Elijah said softly, with a voice of condemnation.

"It's a matter of life and death," Lao said urgently as Elijah raised an eyebrow.

"That's not our concern." Elijah walked back to his table with no remorse.

"I think Branch is going to kill someone." Lao watched him with controlled fierceness.

"What's that to you?" Elijah said passively. "Many people in our position have exacted revenge on their own. He isn't the first and he won't be the last."

"But..." Lao said forming fists in his pants pocket.

"Do not get involved, Lao, or it will only make things worse," Elijah said paternally. "If you get in the way, it will come after your loved ones."

"But what if Branch is going after a loved one already?"

Elijah's eyes seemed distant as he looked in Lao's. "You have to learn to handle their deaths. If you don't learn to control your urges, more will come," Elijah said as he walked away. "More will come," he mouthed as he headed back to his coffee-drinking acquaintances.

"Can you at least tell me if you know where he lives?"

Elijah didn't stop but waved him goodbye.

Lao watched in disbelief as his searching seemed fruitless. He turned to leave as the cashier by the door was counting her drawer.

"What's wrong, kiddo?" she asked, sticking a pencil in her hair as a pin to keep her bun in place.

"I'm looking for someone."

"Everyone comes into Pop's," said the fifty-year-old woman with a warm smile. "Who are you looking for?" She closed her drawer and printed her cash receipt giving Lao her undivided attention.

"Do you know of a guy named Branch?" Lao asked timidly, knowing that even though they lived in a small town, the chances were slim.

"That's not a common name." She scrunched her nose while chewing on her peppermint gum.

"I know," he grimaced, his feeling of hope dwindling.

"Well, that makes things much easier then," she grinned. "Branch Harlow is the owner of the gym off of Huckleberry Street. Do you know where that's at?"

Lao grinned with a renewal of hope. "Thank you!" He darted out the door almost colliding with a couple of patrons coming into Pop's. "Excuse me. Sorry."

He knew there could be another Branch, but he wondered what the chances were that an avid runner was also a gym owner. He thought they were pretty high.

CHAPTER 46

Lao ran across town, jaywalking across the city streets hoping he could find the two men he was looking for. He got to Elite Fitness and found the door locked. He pounded on the glass door, but it appeared no one was inside.

He ran around the building and saw the back parking lot was empty as well. Branch wasn't here, but he had a name.

He pulled out his phone and searched for his home address. In less than a minute, Lao had the directions to Branch's country home near the city limits three miles away.

Lao sprinted to Branch's address and was there in a little over fifteen minutes. His immortality had its benefits every once in a while. The house was a reddish-brown brick three-bedroom ranch home with hunter green window shutters that matched the garage door behind the house.

Lao ran up the driveway and saw a vehicle with a 13.1 window decal parked in front of the detached garage. "Branch!" Lao sprinted to the side screen door. "Branch!" His fist pounded on the glass as he kept screaming. "Branch!"

Lao peeked through the glass, looking around the living room for any sign of Phil. There wasn't anything that looked suspicious, except Branch not coming to the door.

Lao continued to pound on the door, but still Branch never emerged.

Lao walked away from the side door and examined the setting of Branch's home. He had shut all the window blinds around the house, sealing out any light and protecting his privacy from prying eyes.

Lao screamed Branch's name as he ran around the home. Still, he never showed himself.

Is Phil with you? Lao quickly texted to Thya and Smyrna who both replied no. He rushed back to Branch's car and touched the hood. It was still warm from a morning drive. He walked around the car and looked through the passenger windows. He saw something familiar.

Phil's backpack was on the floor.

"Branch!" Lao looked at the house and then at the garage. Opening the driver's side door, he found the garage door opener attached to the visor. He clicked the three buttons, and the garage door slowly rose as a whistle sounded from inside.

"Phil!"

"Branch, just let him go. He probably doesn't even know he hit you."

"I hit him?" Phil murmured but it only sounded like an agonized moan.

"See! He didn't even know he hit you!" Lao tried to deescalate the situation the best he could as Phil slithered away from Branch.

"Stop!" Branch lurched as he pointed the gun at Phil's head, moving the cigarette to his mouth so he could grip the gun with both hands. "Don't move!"

"Branch, think about it. Do you want to go to prison for killing him? I'm a witness and you can't kill me."

"Huh?" Phil screeched in surprise as another shadow spread behind Lao, causing his body to freeze and his ears to sting from a high-pitched whistle. The dark shadow moved quickly to Phil's tangled body.

Lao moved his eyes to look at Branch holding the gun, but it now looked like he froze as well. Branch's hand was flexing and twitching, his finger tickling the trigger.

Phil rolled around on his back, scooting closer to the wall and farther away from the barrel of the gun. He rolled until he collided with the wall, causing the sharp garden tools above him to shake.

Lao's eyes darted over to Phil. He wanted to save his friend, but he couldn't do anything but watch. He felt a coldness that cut to his core. The knives and axes over Phil's head danced along the wall, clicking and clanking against one another, as if sharpening by their scuffs.

Lao wanted to look over at Branch, but his eyes were locked on Phil who was trying his best to cut the ropes tied around his hands against a shovel lying on the ground. Lao watched as he saw threads splinter and fray.

Phil looked up at Lao, begging for help. Lao felt like a prison guard about to witness an execution. He felt sick as he wondered who was the one causing this death.

Phil continued to grind the rope against the shovel until he made a sudden sharp movement freeing his hands, causing the shovel to glide across the smooth concrete and hit a table leg beside the lawn mower. He reached up and took out the gag from his mouth.

"Lao! Help me! Help me! Why are you just standing there!"

Lao looked past Phil helplessly as he saw the table teeter back and forth, trying to stabilize. Suddenly, one angel kicked the table leg, causing all the contents to fall over. The gas cans toppled, spilling the liquid on the floor. It gushed like a waterfall as its new river created a path toward Phil.

Phil didn't even notice the liquid spreading until he felt the lake of gasoline hit his seat. His blue jeans soaked up the gasoline like a cactus refueling itself from a desert storm. The gas continued to spread, filling the entire garage floor, except for a protective circle around Lao and Branch.

Lao's eyes looked past Phil's as he saw a mirror image of Branch's lips quiver in the shiny axe hanging above Phil's head, causing a flaming cigarette to fall from uncontrolled lips.

Lao watched in horror as Phil's eyes widened in realization as the fragile cigarette hit the gasoline, causing a ravenous fire. The yellow and red flames spread faster than Phil could scream.

But he still screamed as Lao watched.

Until Phil screamed no more.

Branch and Lao walked away from the flame as their bodies' tension eased.

Lao couldn't look back at his former friend. The angel had already left.

"Were you forced to watch it?" Lao asked Branch as the flame continued to burn, engulfing his entire garage.

"Huh?" he asked baffled by what just happened.

"Could you look away as he was dying?"

He nodded his head yes. "I unted ta atch."

I wanted to watch.

CHAPTER 48

Lao stayed around with Branch as they waited for the police, who labeled it a horrific accident. Neither one told the true story of how Phil got into the garage. Lao said they were at Branch's house for an early morning workout and then Phil accidentally caused a fire and died.

Parts were true.

By time the police arrived, the fire had burned any fragments of rope away with no trace. The police would have found traces if they investigated, but since Lao was a friend of Phil's, they decided to not investigate it as a crime.

The police were the last to leave after the coroner took Phil's body and the firefighters extinguished the fire. Branch stood in his driveway, staring at the rubble of burnt wood and hot metal.

Lao didn't know if he needed to stay with Branch, but he didn't feel like going to school and lying to his friends. The two stood staring at what used to be.

Branch would occasionally look over at Lao, wanting to ask a question, but he didn't know where to start the inquisition. Lao would look over at Branch wishing the other man was at fault for Phil's death, but he knew that ultimately, it was his own.

He was the one who caused everything to spiral with one sentence. It was a phrase he hoped he would never say again.

You can't kill me.

Those four words caused the first domino to fall. It was Lao's fault, even though he was trying to save Phil. It only took one tiny weight to unbalance the scales of mortality. Those four little words caused the balance to come unhinged with a violent spark.

Lao broke one rule when he told someone he was an immortal. By breaking a rule, the angel of death pounced in retribution.

His angel of death.

He killed Phil. Not Branch.

It was Lao's fault, and he knew it.

CHAPTER 49

Lao's mom was waiting on the couch when he entered the quiet apartment.

"Sit down, Lao," she said solemnly. "I want to talk to you."

Lao pulled off his backpack, setting it on the floor as he sat in the recliner. "Okay. Talk."

"Lao, how are you doing?" she asked compassionately. It was a sympathetic emotion he wasn't used to seeing in his mother. She was a nurse who dealt with sick and dying patients daily. Death was just a part of the cycle of life. When he was six, she had the death talk with him after his hamster died when it got loose in the apartment and the vacuum sucked it up. She was straight and to the point. Shedding no tears. No words of mercy. Just straight facts that things die and you move on.

"I'm okay," he said uncomfortably as if she were going to have the sex talk with him next, a talk that would be delivered too late.

The two sat in silence. His mother gazed longingly at Lao for a word. Lao knew she was staring at him even though he fixed his eyes on his fingers fiddling with the loose threads on the armchair. He felt the gaping distance between them as the haunting silence filled the room like a layer of smoke. A heavy fog that seemed to grow denser with each second that passed.

"Don't you want to talk about it?" she asked with a raspy voice, leaning forward from the couch, trying to look her son in his eyes with tears forming in her own. "He was your friend, Lao. This has to hurt."

Stay jaded. Stay jaded. Stay jaded.

"Death happens," he said flatly still watching his fingers twirl the brown aging threads. "Can I go?" He leaned down to get his bag between his feet, focusing his eyes on his shoes and not the shadow.

"No." She shook her head. "I see things like this at work when people don't express themselves. If they just keep it bottled up, then more damage will come."

He smiled to himself and thought. *Actually, keeping it bottled up will lessen the damage.*

"How're Thya and Smyrna doing?"

That little question spurred an avalanche of emotions. He swung in one instant from aloof to judgmental. "How do you know about Thya? I've never mentioned her to you. Have you been looking at my phone again?" he snapped. "I told you to not invade my privacy!"

"Leonardo, don't talk to me that way!"

"Why not?" he shouted back. "You do it to me all the time. How does it feel? And say my name right!"

She started to cry as her head fell into her shaking hands.

Lao didn't know if this was a trick, because in all his years with his mother, he had only seen her cry a few times. He didn't think this situation was worthy of her shedding tears.

"Your school called me, Lao," she said with fragility in her words, shaking her head. "Your school called me and said your friend died. A friend I didn't know about. Then they told me about your girlfriend and her friend who was Phil's girlfriend and I just fell apart, Lao." Her tears flowed freely. "What have I done to you for you to stay so far away from me?"

Lao looked at his crumbling mother and didn't know what to say. She was just a few feet away, but through the years they had drifted apart like icebergs in the ocean. He didn't want to go through the countless times when he'd felt like a mistake. He didn't want to open his mental journal entries of times when he'd wanted to run away. He didn't want to say how many times his mother had failed him.

"Lao, say something," she said, her voice breaking into a million little pieces. "Anything."

Lao watched. He didn't know what to say. He didn't want to lie to her and tell her she was the best mother in the world. Even she knew she would never win that prize unless she was running against a meth-addict mother who sold her kid for a hit.

"I don't know what to say," Lao said, holding onto his backpack strap, wanting to flee the living room for the privacy of his bedroom.

"Tell me about your friends. Tell me anything. What's your favorite memory of Phil? Do you have any pictures of Thya? I bet she's pretty, because you are so handsome. And so kind." She stopped as her face fell into her trembling hands to catch her falling tears. "I don't deserve a kid like you. I don't deserve you, *Laonardo.*"

Lao dropped his backpack strap and jumped over to the couch to console his broken mother. He didn't want to sweep aside all the pieces broken in their past, but he didn't want to keep them on the mantle as a reminder of their messy relationship either.

Lao opened up. He started speaking from his heart about Thya's smile. How he only befriended Phil because Thya was friends with him. He laughed about the time when they went to Frost's and none of them had enough money for ice cream so they worked the counter for an hour to pay for their sundae. "Walter said if we wanted nuts and whipped cream we would have to work another hour," he grinned.

"So, did you?"

"Of course," he smiled as a tear rolled down his cheek. "How can you have a sundae without nuts and whipped cream?"

"You are my son after all." She wiped away a tear as her mascara ran down her cheeks like tire marks as a smile broke through her rough exterior.

"I guess so," he smiled as he too wiped away a tear.

He closed his eyes and hugged his mother as a light whistle sounded between his ears. He didn't want to open his eyes, but he knew he had to find out where it was. His head was on her shoulder when he saw the shadow appear on the couch beside her, inches from his face.

Quit crying! Quit crying! Quit crying!

He stood up and tried to pull away from his mother's embrace, but she wouldn't let go. Her hand slid down his arm until all she could hold was his fingertips. He looked down and saw her hanging onto her proverbial last thread as he teetered on a cliff inside his own mind.

A whistle blared, louder than he had ever heard. He tipped backwards, feeling his hand free from her grip. He felt like he was falling into an ocean of confusion. He looked up at the speckled ceiling as the whistling resounded like a disastrous symphony.

Stop!

Lao screamed to himself. Suddenly, it was like he rebounded, hurrying his foot to catch his falling self. He looked up at the ceiling and the falling sensation passed as quickly as it came. His dizziness stopped and he stood up straight like nothing was wrong. The whistling had even quieted down to a soft hum.

He went to his bedroom and closed the door behind him. He waited to see the shadow in the corner, but it didn't follow him into his bedroom. He grabbed his phone and texted Thya, hoping she would quit giving him the cold shoulder.

He waited for ten minutes, but she didn't respond.

He waited another five minutes, watching the corner as if sitting in a tree stand at five in the morning waiting for the perfect deer to walk into view. No deer came by and neither did the shadow.

He stepped out of his room and his body froze when he found his mom sleeping on the couch as the angel of death stood leaning over her. Its draping cloth hovered inches over her mouth, moving like a dancer with each of her exhales.

The whistler was watching Lao's mother sleep with its twisted finger hovering over her forehead.

CHAPTER 50

Lao's body wasn't frozen from the angel, but because his own fear got the better of him.

Stay calm. Stay calm. Stay calm.

The angel straightened up and watched keenly as Lao stood on the other side of the room. He kept repeating the two words over and over as he went back to his bedroom. He watched the corner where the shadow usually resided, hoping it would eventually come in.

He needed to find his center, to control his emotions. He picked up his cell phone and called his grandmother. He waited for her to pick up, but she never did. It went straight to voicemail.

"Hey, Grandma, it's me, Lao. I just wanted to see if I could go to church with you sometime. I think you sometimes go in the middle of the week." He stopped and looked around the room as the corner turned dark. "I want to go with you. So, if you can tell me when you go, I'll meet you."

He ended his call and hoped she would call back immediately. He waited fifteen minutes before calling again, leaving another message.

"Hey Grandma, it's me again. Just wanted to make sure you got my message. I really need to speak with someone about this God thing. So, if you can call me back. Thanks."

He once again ended his call and waited.

And waited.

And waited.

The last twenty-four hours had been so strange. His girlfriend was upset with him. His mother, who he thought never liked him, was friendly. And his grandmother, who always wanted to see him, wasn't taking his calls or returning them.

It was just like everything had flipped upside down.

His phone went off, indicating he received a text. He smiled with the thought of Thya finally texting him back.

It wasn't her.

This news may come to you bittersweet, but the district has decided not to redo the 200 meter freestyle race since you were so far in the lead before, you know. Well, congratulations, Lao. You won district. The rest of the races will be this Saturday. Coach Haman.

He reread the phone but didn't feel excited. He felt like he had cheated his way to first place. It wasn't the rest of the swimmers' fault he was invincible now. It just didn't seem fair.

His phone chimed again with another text. This time it was from Thya.

How are you doing? I can't imagine what you're going through. Smyrna and I are going to meet at Pop's tomorrow morning before heading to the funeral home for the visitation. She is devastated. I think it will be good if you can show up.

Lao smiled as he quickly responded saying he would be there. He reread her text a dozen times while he waited for her to respond. Suddenly, his phone chimed with multiple texts from Thya, and he felt ten times better.

The shadow in the corner started to swell.

CHAPTER 51

The barn was lively and energetic when Lao walked in. He put on his green robe and mingled with other immortals like it was an eternal costume party where everyone dressed alike.

Lao caught Elijah looking his direction from across the barn. He didn't know if the look was good or bad, but he felt various eyes on him as if marking him.

Walter walked up and started talking about his latest conquest with a long pair of legs that was nothing short of 'kingdom come'. Lao tried to be friendly, nodding and smiling, but he couldn't erase the feeling of uncertainty surrounding him.

I thought this was a safe place, he thought, but he suddenly didn't feel very safe as Branch hobbled in and various group members surrounded him with love and smiles.

Lao looked over at the small gathering and eavesdropped as well as he could. He couldn't make out much, but he saw various group members patting Branch on his back.

"What's that about?" Lao asked Walter who turned his head to see the commotion.

Walter turned his head back to Lao with a cunning smile. "You tell me."

"Tell you what?" Lao asked in defense.

"Come off it," he laughed. "Everyone knows what you did."

"What *I* did?" Lao balked, scanning the room as if looking for a place to escape other than the door Branch was standing beside.

"You know," Walter grinned as he walked away, leaving his judgment at Lao's feet.

Lao was alone. If he was at any other party he would have migrated to the table for a drink, but as an immortal, drinks weren't needed. He stood awkwardly alone with nothing to do but watch and wait.

He watched as Elijah continued to socialize, but he never stepped over that invisible line to head Lao's way. He felt like no one was going to step over that line the rest of the night.

He felt a tap on his shoulder from behind. "We need to talk."

CHAPTER 52

"Don't turn around," the stranger whispered in his ear. "Meet me behind the farmhouse in thirty minutes."

Lao nodded his head as he continued to watch the various groups meshing together. The stranger walked away with his hood up, moving through the crowd, getting lost in the plethora of green robes.

Lao looked down at his phone to get the time, wondering why the secrecy. But he knew. The stranger didn't want to be seen fraternizing with the so-called enemy.

Lao swallowed his fear and stepped across the invisible line. He smiled and listened to people's conversations, but he never said a word. He just floated in and out of groups, killing time before he could sneak off.

He heard Elijah laughing in the distance, carefree and full of vigor. He longed for the day when he could tell a joke and share a wonderful memory without knowing he had to watch someone die. He hoped he would get there. But Elijah had many more years under his belt partaking in this mixed-up existence.

Minutes were trickling by as if Lao was watching an hourglass of sand. He knew the time was almost up. He peered his head down to look at his phone when a voice whispered into his ear.

"Ow'd you ow?

How'd I know? Lao turned around to look Branch in his lopsided eye.

The look of confusion and disheartenment hit Lao like a tidal wave of remorse. He didn't answer but became keenly aware that if he and Phil had taken an extra minute to look for the presumably dying deer, Branch would have died and ended his existence as a ruggedly handsome, personal trainer who probably had more definition in his abs and chest at forty than Lao had in his high-testosterone fueled adolescence with spiking metabolism.

But now, Branch was as broken as his namesake after a storm. A fallen tree limb twisted and mangled from the winds of a violent tornado. But it wasn't a tornado that wrecked him.

It was Phil's car.

But it wasn't all Phil's fault. Lao could have stepped off the road into the darkened grass to find a bleeding man, moaning for death to take him quickly.

Lao wondered if Branch still moaned for death to take him.

He wondered if looking at his photos from Saturday night felt like a lifetime away. In one instant, the image he had been perfecting since the first time he stepped into a gym in high school was all over. His arms were still toned, but the muscles were now detached and displaced in unorthodox locations on his arm. His dream of competing in the Iron Man Triathlon was now as close to coming true as leaving this nightmare.

Lao closed his eyes and wiped them so Branch couldn't see a tear falling. He turned his head and answered because he couldn't stand to look into his eyes any longer.

"I don't know," he lied.

He felt the punch to his gut for such a blatant lie.

He walked away to get to the door; his thirty minutes were up. He had lied to the man he helped kill. Even though he wasn't driving, he didn't help the situation.

"Dive afe," Branch said sinisterly to Lao. "Ou evr know ut ay appen."

Lao stopped and wondered, was that a threat?

Drive safe. You never know what may happen.

If it wasn't a threat, it sure was a remark of suspicion.

CHAPTER 53

Lao walked through the small forest as his accompanying angel of death lurked behind, following his every move like an awe-struck little brother. He came to the clearing and headed up the dirt path toward the farmhouse. He looked behind him, eyeing the scene for any followers.

He was alone.

He walked up the path as it got darker with the increasing clouds in the sky. The wind increased as a storm was rolling into the town of Sardis.

The front porch appeared welcoming with a three-seat swing tossing in the wind. The chains clanked and squeaked as if saying hello.

Lao walked past the sleeping home, peeking his eyes through the window glimpsing nothing but blinds covering the windowpanes. He had always wanted to live in a home like this. Out in the country with some land where he could sleep without hearing his neighbors' televisions. He reached out his hand and felt the whitewashed vinyl siding and imagined living in a home in his future.

His future was limitless now.

He turned around the corner and found a stranger sitting in an aluminum green chair under a sturdy oak tree. He still couldn't make out who the dark stranger was in the tree's shade.

"I'm glad you came," the stranger said as he waved Lao to come closer and have a seat.

Lao didn't recognize the voice. He waited for his vision to adjust to the darkness to make out the stranger's face. Slowly, his eyes saw the outline as his profile showcased a long pointy noise.

"Before we start, let me introduce myself." The gentleman reached into his pocket and pulled out a lighter and new cigar. He flicked the lighter causing a small flame to cut through the darkness.

"My name is Judah," he said puffing on his cigar to get a strong light, licking his lips imagining the earthy taste.

The light showed the face of a man who appeared to become an immortal in his early forties. His smile was forced, as if manufactured to gain Lao's trust. His brown eyes matched his short brown hair, and his skin radiated a soft glow.

Lao nodded his head as he sat down in the adjacent chair. "Nice to meet you." He wondered what else to say. He had many questions he wanted to ask, but he was going to be patient. Judah had approached him.

"You may be wondering why I wanted to speak to you while we are not protected by the forces of the barn."

Lao nodded.

"Well, I don't know how to tell you this, but some of those people in that barn," he stopped and leaned back with his cigar between his stained fingers, "can't be trusted."

Lao twisted his mouth in confusion. "Why not?"

"Well, no matter how much they try to tell you they care about you, don't believe them." He stopped and blew out two rings of smoke.

Lao watched the floating circles as they quickly vanished with the wind.

"Why should I trust you and not them?"

"Maybe you shouldn't," he winked. "But that's for you to decide."

Lao wiggled in his chair as he felt a coldness he hadn't felt in the barn. His shadow rested between the two of them.

"Why shouldn't I trust them?"

Judah took a deep puff and talked freely as he ignored the shadow, taking in every word he said.

"What they didn't tell you, Lao, is they know a way to keep their loved ones a little safer."

"And what is that?" Lao leaned closer and took in every word.

"Well, what if I say they use new immortals' friends and family as their sacrificial lambs? How would you feel if they know how to trade their friends for your friends?"

Lao looked dumbstruck. "But they said…"

"Yes," Judah nodded as if that was a crucial piece of the puzzle. "They said." He stopped and looked up into the tree limbs above him. "But who's to say what they said was true?"

"Are you saying I'm not immortal?" Lao asked as shock and disbelief swirled like hot and cold air.

"Oh, no," he laughed. "You did die. And they didn't lie when they said your angel of death will act out in revenge because it wants lives to take. But the question is, does your angel really only want to take the lives of *your* friends and family?" He stopped and looked Lao in his eyes. "Or will your angel of death take any lives to satisfy its desire?"

Judah stopped and let those words sink in.

"Think, Lao, who has died around you lately? Are they really your closest friends and family or just people you know?" He stopped and reclined once again. "Just think about it. Who was the first person who died in your presence?" He stopped. "Or *what* was?"

Lao thought back over the last few days.

"A bird died first," he answered. "I was mesmerized and couldn't take my eyes off it as it was dying."

Judah grinned. "And were you close to that bird?"

Lao shook his head.

"So, if the angel was only acting out revenge on living things close to you, why did it take a bird?" He stopped for a second to let the question simmer. "Because the angel of death doesn't care. It just wants death. It doesn't care who is killed as long as it gets to savor it."

"Why?" Lao's brain spun as his beliefs before this night started to split and ricochet. "Why did they lie to me?"

"Think about it, Lao," he said casually. "If someone tells you something not to do, what is your first inclination?"

"To do it."

"Exactly. So, when they told you the angel of death would kill all of your friends and family, who were you thinking about?" He stopped and answered the question. "Your friends and family, right?"

Lao nodded his head.

"And when you think of your friends and family dying, how does that make you feel? Sad? Depressed? Angry? Hurt?" Judah stopped and knocked some of his ashes from his cigar. "All the emotions the angel of death loves to inflict, right?"

Lao once again nodded his head.

"So, if they can get you to dwell on all those thoughts, that will cause your angel of death to strike more often. If your angel of death strikes more often, it will cause their angels not to. It may sound strange, and I don't understand it all, but once I quit believing them, I started being much, much happier."

Lao turned his head to look behind him, watching his back for a sudden attack.

"Why are you telling me? Don't you want my friends to die so yours won't?"

"Kid, I've been around for a few thousand years," he said flatly. "You may think being immortal is going to be great, but it's not. So if I can help one person on this cruel, sick journey, well, it's worth it." He puffed on his cigar and smiled devilishly. "And if it causes Elijah and his friends some pain, well it just makes it worth so much more."

Lao kept his guard up. "But, why are you telling me?"

"Because you're not like them, kid," Judah said shrugging his shoulders. "At least, I don't think you are. I saw how the entire room was watching you tonight like you betrayed them."

"But I didn't!" Lao exclaimed as he quickly covered his mouth and lowered his volume. "I didn't betray anyone."

"Well, every one of these groups has a leader, and here it's Elijah," he said flatly. "And when you didn't follow his orders today, well, you were moved to the blacklist."

"The blacklist?" Lao said in disgust. "I was just trying to help Branch not kill someone and go to jail."

"Yeah, they are pissed you messed that up," he laughed. "One of the other members was the one who helped track down the person who hit him."

"Why? Why do they care? Why did they want him to go to jail? I thought they would want to protect him."

"Think, Lao." Judah leaned forward and stared into Lao's eyes. "Thousands of people in one place that encompasses so much hate, fear, dread, and pain. It's an angel of death playground. If they could have gotten Branch to go there and suffer for fifteen years, that would have been fifteen years of them not having to worry about their friends and family."

Lao's eyes widened as he realized what he had done without knowing it.

"So now they're having to think up something new," he said casually. "So yeah, kid, you're going to be on the blacklist for a very long time." Judah smiled. "Welcome to the club."

CHAPTER 54

Twilight was approaching as the stars and moon glowed in their splendor, as if they knew they would soon be saying goodbye. Lao drove away from the farm house, leaving Branch's car still parked on the side of the road. That thought alarmed him as he wondered why he was still there.

He drove home with his high-beams on his mother's vehicle, watching out for darting deer that seemed drawn to speeding cars. Occasionally, he would see a pair of eyes in the darkness. The eyes didn't run away but watched him as if following his move.

The longer he drove, the more he thought the eyes were not that of deer. *What if the eyes were of them?*

As he gripped the steering wheel, fear crept in with a feeling of entanglement. He was afraid their strings would eventually tie him up for an eternity. He wasn't fearful of choking. He was fearful of not. Because enduring an eternity on the outskirts with this group of people would be a very long time without a community to find solace with.

He turned sharply, waking up from his dream state of what-ifs and morbid possibilities, doing his best to keep the vehicle on the road. His back tires skidded off the road, losing traction with the pavement as it slid off of the embankment into a grassy side while he slammed on the brake.

He tried to correct the vehicle, but like most drivers, over-corrected. He felt the vehicle spin. He watched as the headlights shone into the distance as multiple pairs of eyes watched.

But once again, they were not the eyes of terrified deer watching from the distance.

They looked more like the eyes of a hunter with his scope set on a target.

He felt like he was wearing a bullseye.

The car leaned on the passenger side, as he felt a flip was imminent. He closed his eyes and hoped for the car to stop. Lao felt it slow as it shifted its weight back onto all four tires. He was afraid to open his eyes, but he felt it was safe.

The tension remained in his arms as he continued to clutch the steering wheel with a deadly grip. He let out a deep breath, not because his immortal lungs needed it, but out of habit. After turning off the ignition, he sat for a minute to let his nerves calm while his headlights continued to shine into the distance.

He looked out ahead and squinted his eyes but saw nothing but a streak of sunlight breaking through the nighttime sky.

He turned the ignition and pressed the brake pedal to switch into drive. Looking in his rearview mirror, he saw multiple pairs of eyes reflecting in the red light. He could even make out a face. It looked like Enoch's.

He twisted his head but nothing was there. The eyes were gone. The face disappeared. He was alone.

He turned back around and drove forward as he looked into the rearview mirror. Once again, multiple pairs of eyes were watching from the distance. They looked like they were moving forward as if on the front lines of a military battle. He didn't want to look anymore, but he couldn't take his eyes off the mirror. The longer he looked, the closer they got to his vehicle. He started to make out multiple faces, but he couldn't see the detailed features. He just knew they weren't deer. They were definitely humans.

A feeling of ambush was embedding in his stomach as the eyes moved in closer.

Along with a pair of speeding headlights.

CHAPTER 55

The headlights were coming closer. Lao watched in suspense as the vehicle sped down the two-lane road as if trying to outrun the breaking sunlight.

Lao hit the gas. The engine revved with a force that growled like a lion. His tires skidded as they tried to connect with the pavement. He started driving away and looked in the rearview mirror.

There wasn't anyone anymore. The eyes vanished as if they hadn't been there a minute ago.

Were they there? he asked himself as he continued to drive into the dawn as the navy sky started to change to a purplish shade with a piece of the sun poking its face over the horizon like a losing game of peek-a-boo.

He watched as the car behind him was speeding up. It was coming closer.

It's probably somebody late for work, he tried to tell himself, but he needed something more than his hopeful words as reassurance. He needed to be right.

His speedometer was rising, teetering on 85 miles per hour, thirty over the speed limit for this state route. He had forgotten about the deer escaping the rifle fire of hunting season. He wasn't watching on both sides of the road for that sudden jolt of seeing a rack of antlers inches in front of the vehicle, hurdling into the windshield. He wasn't thinking of anything but the car chasing him.

The sun was steadily rising, shining into the darkest regions of his mind and the farmland nearby. Both were desolate now. Harvest season had taken all the crops, leaving only a tilled field waiting for the next round of seeds. His mind was just as barren. He'd thought he could trust Elijah like a grandfather. He'd thought the group was a place where he could learn new qualities such as trust and loyalty.

But Judah had dismantled all his preconceived notions with a little honesty. Or maybe Judah was hoping his loyalties would shift to him.

Lao sat confused. His hands were gripping the steering wheel as it shook from the speed of the vehicle as the speedometer moved past ninety. It gyrated and vibrated like a massaging pad, but it didn't make him feel any better.

It only made him realize how easily things could slip through his fingers.

The speeding car was catching up from behind. Lao squinted his eyes and saw there was only one person in the driver's seat.

Lao saw the city of Sardis coming into his vision. He didn't know why seeing the quiet little town caused a smile to appear on his face, but he started to feel safe. As if nothing bad could happen in the daylight hours beside the library and Russell's Hardware store.

He slowed as he approached the red light at the intersection. He watched with bated breath as the car behind him didn't appear to slow. He didn't care about the red light anymore. He was entranced by the headlights behind him.

The speeding car was almost at his bumper when it swerved to Lao's left, pulling up beside him at the light, stopping in the lane heading the wrong direction.

Lao looked over at the driver who was wearing a pair of reflective sunglasses.

"Follow me," the driver said with his passenger-side window down.

"Huh?" Lao asked as he timidly rolled his window down.

"Follow me." As the light turned green, he spun his tires and darted in front of Lao, getting in the correct driving lane.

Lao didn't know what to do.

The only saving grace was a morbid thought as he drove, following the familiar-looking stranger.

Well, at least he can't kill me.

CHAPTER 56

The driver pulled into the Ephesus Manufacturing parking lot, a run-down furniture manufacturer that went out of business during the last president's administration when the jobs were shipped overseas and had remained vacant ever since. Lao pulled in beside him and waited for what to do. The driver got out and walked up to his car, so Lao cracked the window. Lao wondered if the smell of wood grains and varnish still wafted through the air as if the factory had never shut down.

The driver bent down to speak through the crack.

"What do you think you are doing talking to him?"

"Who?" Lao asked innocently as his voice cracked in that one syllable word.

"Are you kidding me?" He shook his head as he burst into uncontrollable laughter. "Lying to my face as I'm trying to help you?"

Lao sat in the car with one hand on the steering wheel and the other on the gear stick.

"Why shouldn't I talk to him?" Lao blurted out like a teenager questioning his parent.

"Because you shouldn't trust him." The stranger stepped closer to the car, pointing his finger at Lao.

"Why?"

"Just believe me." He walked away shaking his head, looking at his wrist watch.

"Why?" Lao shouted as he turned off his car and opened the door. "Why should I believe *you*?" he asked, catching up to the stranger as he was getting into his vehicle. "I don't even know your name."

"You don't know his either."

"He told me his name was Judah," Lao said as he caught the stranger's car door before it shut.

"Kid, he's been every name in the book at least once," he said turning the ignition of his vehicle. "You're just the newest pawn in his game."

"Game? This isn't a game. This is my life!"

The stranger smiled with a slight chuckle. "It may be your life, but it's just a game to him." He stopped and looked up at Lao through his sunglasses. "And Cain doesn't like to lose."

Lao stared at him more confused than ever and his reflection in his glasses confirmed it.

He closed the door and was about to pull away when he rolled down his window. "Benjamin."

"Huh?"

"My name," he said shaking his head. "My name is Benjamin."

"I'm…" he started before Benjamin interrupted.

"I know who you are, Lao. We all know who you are." He pulled away leaving Lao standing in the broken pavement with cracks and crevices. He had heard stories of married men coming here to meet up with their mistresses or people getting a few grams of cocaine for a decent price. There were rumors that illegals used to live in the break room, but they were never confirmed.

He now felt like those supposed illegals. He wanted to hide because he didn't know who he could trust. But hiding wasn't an option, per Elijah.

Or was Judah telling the truth? Or Cain? Or whatever his name was.

Or was Benjamin?

CHAPTER 57

Lao returned home and dropped off the car before his mother found out about his nighttime adventures. He ran into the apartment to grab his backpack when Thya invited him to breakfast at Pop's with her and Smyrna.

Please come, she texted, *for Smyrna.*

I'll be there, Lao replied.

Lao found the two girls sitting quietly on the same side of the table, each with a coffee in her hand. He scanned the restaurant and found Elijah sitting in the corner with the old men of the town. Lao expected Elijah to give him the evil eye as he walked by, but he never even looked up from the newspaper in his hands.

"How are you two doing?" Lao asked, sitting down to see a mirror hanging on the wall between Smyrna and Thya along with a collection of old lawn and garden antiques hanging sporadically on the ceiling and walls.

"I still can't believe it," Thya clutched her warm cup of coffee with her frigid hands looking into it for some solace.

"Me either," Lao said, looking over at Smyrna in condolence.

"Did he say anything?" Smyrna asked, looking up from her steaming cup with weary, bloodshot eyes.

"He..." Lao stopped and moved his eyes between the two of them. "He didn't have time."

"Just tell me he didn't suffer." Thya looked across the table, almost begging Lao to ease their minds and hearts.

Lao shook his head. "He didn't suffer." He didn't want to reflect any more than he had to, but luckily the fire overtook Phil quickly. He may have suffered for a minute, but his clothes sucked up the gas igniting him like a firework. He didn't want to think of someone dying, but the angel of death wanted him badly. He wasn't taking any chances on Phil diverting death.

The waitress came up and took their breakfast order leaving the three to sit in grieving silence.

Lao looked between the girls and noticed a pair of eyes watching him from the mirror. Elijah had found him.

Lao didn't turn around or acknowledge Elijah's existence. Lao knew if he approached the old man, he would just lift his paper again. Elijah was trying to slyly watch Lao, and Lao was doing the same.

The waitress returned with two plates of pancakes and Smyrna's steak and eggs.

"Oh, let me get you a knife for that steak," the waitress said as she rushed away.

Thya poured her hot buttery syrup over her three pancakes, but her eyes didn't look hungry. They looked tired and wearisome. Lao watched as a handyman climbed a ladder, replacing a few of the burned-out light bulbs a few tables over. Lao felt a chill fill the air as the angel of death strutted into the room and a shadow seeped into the room.

"Watch out!" the handyman shouted as he dropped a package of light bulbs, smashing them to the ground, breaking the fragile bulbs into a thousand little glass pieces.

"Whoa!" the waitress exclaimed as she walked through carrying a steak knife in her hand without seeing the slippery glass pieces on the restaurant floor.

Lao watched in the mirror with wide eyes as the waitress came forward off balance pointing the knife ahead of her. Thya's eyes became more alert as she saw the sharp blade heading in her direction.

Lao wanted to shout, but he couldn't say a word. His eyes darted around the room, the only thing that he could move.

Laughter filled the room as the waitress fell, plunging the knife into the table next to the three of them.

"That was close," she laughed as she pulled the knife from the wood grain.

"A little too close," Thya feebly laughed as she eyed Lao with concern.

"Here's your knife," the waitress grinned, wiping it down with the towel in her apron before handing it to Smyrna. "Need anything else?"

Smyrna cleaned the blade herself with her paper napkin to be safe. "I don't need anything," she said.

"I could use some more syrup." Thya smiled politely as Lao shook his head, realizing he could move.

"You haven't even touched your pancakes," Lao scolded.

"I'll eat them," she said snidely, "or I'll just take them home for later."

"That's probably what I will do," Smyrna said.

Lao looked into the mirror and saw the angel of death standing in the distance near the table of old men. Lao watched as Elijah gripped his paper tighter, almost tearing it at the edges.

Lao continued to watch, focusing solely on Elijah's fear and dread. He hadn't felt this good in a long time and his smile showed.

"What are you smiling at?" Smyrna asked.

Lao didn't take his eyes off of Elijah.

Even as he heard a scream, Lao continued to smile.

CHAPTER 58

Smyrna stood up and yelled. "Watch out!"

Everyone in the restaurant turned their attention to the handyman whose wooden ladder leg broke off at the bottom. The once sturdy ladder on four legs quickly changed to an unstable accident-inducing catastrophe.

The handyman let out a moan of concern as the men at Elijah's table quickly got up to escape harm while still trying to help.

Lao watched as Elijah looked like an animal about to be caught in a trap. He looked around the standing men, unable to say a word. He couldn't scream. He couldn't move. He was just there. Frozen.

Lao finally realized how he always looked at that moment.

Elijah stood as the other men tried to stabilize the ladder while the handyman clung to the top for dear life.

Die! Die! Die! Lao thought as he watched Elijah continue to stand frozen, looking up at the handyman with sadness in his eyes.

"Why are you still sitting?" Thya asked, looking down at Lao in confusion as the waitress walked through the kitchen doors with more syrup in her hand.

Lao tried to turn around, but he was frozen to his seat. He tried to open his mouth, but he wasn't able.

Suddenly, fear elevated to a new level. It was like the rug was pulled from under his feet as he watched Elijah turn his head and smile.

Lao continued to stare into the mirror, trying to watch his surroundings as the handyman jumped off the ladder and rolled onto the ground safely. The ladder teetered on the three legs, swaying back and forth until physics took over.

Or an angel of death took over. The red circle on its face glowed hauntingly as a loud whistle blared into the room.

The waitress looked oblivious to her surroundings, humming a song in her head with a smile on her face as she walked up and slammed the syrup onto the table. The ladder fell backwards, crashing into the wall. It collided with a white rope used as a clothesline hanging various objects along the ceiling. Quickly the once thick cord unwrapped as the strands broke one by one. Snap. Snap. Snap.

Snap.

The rope's tightness disappeared as the objects attached started to fall from the ceiling. Plastic flowerpots with fake daisies fell to the ground. Old rusty hand tools crashed to the ground like a spring shower of spades and shears.

A three-prong pitchfork fell down, but the line suddenly tightened, holding the wooden, splintered handle with a firm grip until gravity's revenge pulled it down with dominant force, swinging the sharp spikes like a pendulum.

Lao watched but couldn't say a word.

Smyrna's eyes widened as she watched the pitchfork coming her direction.

"Look out!" Thya screamed.

The waitress turned around just in time to see her fate.

The angel of death found its next victim.

Blood dribbled down, causing her white apron to turn red where the three prongs sunk deep into her chest. Quickly her embroidered name, Stephanie, was unrecognizable. The waitress fell backwards landing on Lao's pancakes as screams erupted through the restaurant. He looked down and watched her eyes as they looked into his.

Lao could almost make out her humming as her hair laid in the maple syrup.

But she wasn't humming. It was just her last few strained breaths gasping for air.

The waitress let out her last sigh with a bubble of blood escaping her pink lips. Life drained from her eyes. The angel disappeared as it flicked the waitress' forehead. Lao looked up as Smyrna and Thya continued to scream in catastrophic shock, clutching onto one another for support as they looked away from the horrific scene.

Lao jumped up and tried to console them, but they backed away.

"You did it again, Lao," Thya said in disbelief. "You just watched her die like you did Reid."

"But…" Lao started as he turned around and saw everyone in the restaurant running to the waitress on their table except Elijah who waved at Lao with a sinister smile and walked away.

Lao wondered what Elijah was thinking, but he had a good idea.

I warned you, kiddo.

CHAPTER 59

Lao watched Thya and Smyrna leave Pop's as they darted away from him. He tried to talk to them, but they wouldn't listen. Thya had seen it already, and Smyrna believed everything she was saying.

Lao wished her inclination wasn't true, but deep down inside Thya knew more than she knew. He had just floated there and watched Reid drown. Just as he once again sat there and watched the bubbly waitress get pierced to death. Thya knew parts of the truth, but only parts.

Lao went to the nearby park and sat at the bubbling fountain. He hoped the rushing water sound would help with his nagging thoughts, but it didn't. It just made him wish he could pee. Something he hadn't done in days.

He still didn't understand what was going on. He wasn't eating or sleeping, yet his body remained unchanged. He wasn't thirsty, and he didn't even miss the taste of his favorite vanilla Coke. He couldn't taste anything anymore. And even when he ate, he wondered where it went. It just didn't make sense.

The longer he sat, the longer his agitation grew. The more his agitation grew, the less rational this thought process became. And before he knew it, he was pounding on Branch's side door.

He waited for the limping man to open the door as he looked over his shoulder and saw the remnants of where the garage used to be. From the doorsteps he could still make out the char marks of where Phil burned to death on the concrete floor.

"What you want?" he asked through the door without opening it.

"I just want to talk to you," Lao said calmly.

"You want ta alk?" Branch asked divisively furrowing his brow.

"I know you're confused," Lao said patiently as he started to question his own motives for being at Branch's home. "I'm losing it."

"Your osing it!" Branch pounded his fist against the back door. "Don't tell me bout osing it!"

"I know, I know," Lao said apologetically as he looked down at his movable unscathed body with his arms spread wide. "It's not fair! But it's just us now!"

"Huh?" He squinted his eyes at Lao as his disfigured shifted like his face was made of clay.

"Yeah, Branch," Lao stated unfazed. "They are pitting us against one another. They are playing you and they are playing me."

"Ut ou mean?"

"What do I mean?" Lao laughed. "Last night, I was watched and bullied by everyone in the room, and then some stranger, Judah, pulled me aside and said to meet him at the farmhouse. Then when I was leaving there, some other stranger tracked me down and told me to follow him to an empty parking lot," Lao said shaking his head. "And you know what?"

Branch shook his head no from behind the glass.

"They each told me something different."

"Iffrant?"

"Yeah, Branch. And if they're doing that to me, they are probably doing it to you too." Lao stopped and was afraid to ask the next question. But he asked anyway. "Right?"

Branch didn't answer, but unlocked his deadbolt. "Ou etter not be lying ta me," he said as he opened the screen door.

"I promise, Branch," Lao said as he stepped into some foreign terrain. "I'm not lying to you."

It felt nice to actually tell the truth for a change.

CHAPTER 60

"Want anytang ta dink?" Branch asked before he shook his head realizing his blunder. "Orry. Habit."

"Don't worry," Lao smiled as he stayed by the door. "It's a hard habit to break."

"C'm in," Branch hobbled forward to the living room with beautiful black and white photographs of landscapes framed on the wall.

"Stunning pictures," Lao said as he walked slowly behind. "Did you take these?"

Branch nodded a warm smile as he looked at a picture of the painted desert. "Ood memries."

"Looks like you've traveled to some unbelievable places," Lao said as he examined the pictures further.

Branch sat down in his recliner and offered Lao a seat on the couch.

"So, ou dank they are lying to us?"

Lao shrugged his shoulders and gave a downcast gaze. "Someone is lying, but I don't know who." Lao retraced the last few days with conflicting stories from people he thought he could trust at one moment but then acted suspiciously the next. "Has anyone been telling you different stories?"

He nodded his head.

"What did they say?" Lao leaned further into the conversation.

"Well, Eoch wuz nice, but Uben wuz not."

"Yeah, Enoch has been nice to me as well until last night when he just stared at me through the evening. But I don't know of a Reuben."

"Do ou know Gab?"

"Gab?" Lao shook his head. "I don't know most of the people who come each night, but I have noticed that there are some different people each time."

"Me too," Branch agreed with a quizzical look as a loud churning sound started from under the floor. Lao's eyes widened as the floor lightly vibrated. "Don't worry, itz just my heater in da acement."

"Oh, that makes me feel better," Lao grinned. "I thought something was going to be coming up from underneath to get me."

"Ope," Branch smiled warmly. "You're safe."

Lao smiled back. "So you have a basement in this house?" He nodded toward a latch on the floor. "Is that how you get down there?"

Branch nodded his head. "I don't go down dare much," he said casually. "Itz an ol' well da pior owner turned into a cella. It only has an ol' adder dat's shaky and messed up."

"An old well turned into a cellar? Never heard of that before. Cool."

"Want ta see?"

"Sure," Lao said enthused. He wasn't used to seeing a cellar, let alone a home separated from its neighbors with some land. Branch shakily stood up and walked over to the door on the ground. He tried to lift it, but it was too heavy for his broken body.

Lao quickly helped and easily lifted the solid oak door, resting it on the wall behind it.

"Oh man, you can't see the bottom," Lao stood behind Branch peering down the black hole.

"Very ark," Branch commented.

Lao leaned over and saw the rickety old ladder that looked like a death trap for anyone climbing down it. "I don't blame you for not going down there," Lao smiled as he closed the door. "You really have a nice home. Wish I had something like this, but I just live in a crummy apartment with my mom. But maybe one day," he smiled as he helped Branch back to the recliner.

The two continued to share each other's stories over the last few days. Lao told more of the mischievous ways of Elijah and Judith as Branch nodded and agreed in his suspicion of a few other members of the group.

It seemed Lao had never heard of the people Branch spoke with and vice versa. It was like the group had split up in two sides each trying to sabotage the newest members of their secret organization.

Lao listened to Branch talk and wondered if he was being played by Branch. But then he thought Branch was probably thinking the same thing.

The only thing Lao knew was fairly certain, the group probably didn't see a friendship brewing between the two of them.

But to be honest, Lao didn't see a friendship with Branch developing any time soon either. Maybe further down the road they could be friendly toward one another, but it was still too soon. Branch was just a tool he was going to use for the time being.

He just hoped Branch wasn't thinking the same thing.

CHAPTER 61

Lao sat on Branch's couch until noon before he thought he was wearing off his welcome and stood to leave.

"Can I ask a kestion?"

"Sure," Lao said as he once again walked around the living room to look at a few more photographs up close.

"Why ou eally ear?"

The question caught Lao off guard. He suddenly felt the civility gone in one simple question. "Why am I here?" he asked turning around shocked. "To find the truth."

"C'mon," Branch said changing his mood like he was wearing a color-switching ring.

"Really," Lao said flabbergasted. "I wanted to get your opinion on everything."

"Don't lie ta me!" Branch barked out like someone who was bipolar. He was cordial a minute ago and now he was going spastic in accusations and disbelief.

"I'm not lying!" Lao spit out. "I wanted to see if they were messing with you just as they have been messing with me."

Branch slowly stood up, resting all of his weight on his left leg as he stood shaking. "Iar!"

"I'm not a liar!" Lao retorted. "I'm not!"

"Den why lie bout Anold?"

The question smacked Lao on his face. He was a liar. He'd denied knowing Phil Arnold when Branch asked. He did lie to him, but he was trying to protect a friend.

"Ou lied ta me!"

"I didn't mean to lie to you," Lao said stepping back as his back hit the wall. "I was trying to protect a friend," Lao quickly stammered out. "A friend who didn't know he hit you. He didn't know. He thought he hit a deer."

"But he did't 'it a deer," Branch growled venomously. "He 'it me," he said as his voice croaked with pain and sadness. "He 'it me!"

Lao wanted to console the crying man who was falling apart before him, but he knew his compassionate words and actions wouldn't heal anything in Branch's calloused heart. It would probably only spur more hate and revenge.

Branch wiped his tears and looked up.

"You knew," he said fiercely with evil coursing through his eyes.

"Knew what?"

"Ou knew!"

"Knew what, Branch?" What did I know?"

"Ow'd you know he 'it a deer?"

Lao knew Branch's questioning was getting too close to the truth. He was seeing all the dots connecting. All the missing lines were forming a picture of deceit.

"He told me at school the next day he hit a deer," Lao lied.

"Iar!"

"Why would I lie to you?" Lao asked, lying through his teeth.

"But you are!"

"I am not!"

Branch looked down and noticed something familiar. He stared intently as Lao looked down at the ground as well, trying to figure out what was drawing his attention.

"You were dare!"

"I wasn't there," Lao scoffed as he took a side step closer to the door.

"You were! You were dare! Dats ow you know e 'it a deer! Two guys got out an ooked at da car."

"I wasn't there. I promise," Lao lied as he took another step toward the door. "I only know he hit a deer because he told us. You saw someone else, but it wasn't me."

Branch once again looked down as he took a slow step forward.

"Nice shoes, Lao," he said softly.

Lao looked down at his old, ratty shoes. "These are old," he mocked as he took another step toward the door. "I really need to get a new pair. And I need to go home and get ready to go to the funeral home."

"I ramemer now," he smiled wickedly, ignoring Lao's last comments. "Those shoes were dare tat nigh I died."

Lao looked down and saw he was caught. These were the shoes he wore that night. The night Branch died.

Branch was right.

"I got to go." Lao darted to the door, fleeing outside and running away.

Why did you go here? Why?

CHAPTER 62

"What are you doing here?" Thya asked with scornful jadedness as she sat in an armchair near the entrance of Sardis' only funeral home.

"He was my friend too," Lao said standing with fists by his side, a little hostility in his tone. He looked around the empty lobby, checking his volume for this somber environment.

"Friends don't let friends die in front of them," Thya spit out, furrowing her brow like the words were poison. She folded her arms and turned her head to ignore his presence.

"I tried to help him, but it was too late," Lao responded. He watched as she tuned him out. He stood fragile, on the verge of a nervous breakdown. His surroundings were coming undone, and the only thing he knew for certain it would not end any time soon. This was going to be his new state of normal.

Lao looked over at the aloof Thya who stared out the window, watching anything that moved as if watching the nature channel. He turned away and walked the empty corridor. The funeral home usually had a smell of roses and baby breath that commingled with the aroma that could only be named the fragrance of death.

But he couldn't smell the infamous odor. He couldn't inhale the morbidly toxic fumes of chemicals to preserve the body in a somewhat normal state. He couldn't breathe in the smell of saline from the gallons of tears that had fallen onto the dingy pink carpet over the last twenty years.

He signed his name in the registry and entered the room where Phil's parents were standing like concrete statues beside a life-size portrait of their late son and a silver urn. The fire had left very little of Phil, so the family and mortician chose to cremate the remainder.

Phil's parents appeared to be wrestling with the notion of faith while bottled up with a powerful dose of self-righteous anger. It was a combination of opposing forces they were trying their best to keep separate.

Lao watched as he knew the two forces were going to eventually meet. They were going to collide and foam like the Pacific and Indian Ocean. One would win because there cannot be two leaders in a tango. One eventually has to dominate, and the other has to suppress and follow its lead. He just wasn't sure which would triumph—faith or anger.

Lao took a seat on the last pew. He distantly watched as tears were breaking through the rough exterior like the mighty Colorado through the Grand Canyon. It would not take millions of years for the erosion to happen in Phil's parents' lives. It was going to happen much sooner. It wouldn't be a gradual change, a slight cracking of rock. No, it would be monumental devastation like a sculptor's unremorseful chisel.

Realization would soon stab them in their hearts, and the clumps of marble would fall off their shoulders faster than they could catch them. They would soon find themselves in a rubble of what they once had. They would soon find themselves in a mound of history. A person doesn't recover from that type of destruction easily.

Lao feebly waved to Smyrna who almost succumbed to the greeting, but then stopped. Her eyes darted to the door behind Lao as she quickly lowered her head and went back to holding Phil's mother's hand.

Lao turned his head over his shoulder to see what caused Smyrna's sudden distant heart.

Thya walked into the back of the visitation room, showing an unknown visitor the way to the family so he could give his condolences.

Branch.

CHAPTER 63

"I'm so orry for your oss," Branch said though his drooping mouth.

Phil's family listened intently, trying to make out what Branch was saying through his troubled speech. Lao rushed up behind to hear everything being said in case he needed to interject.

"How did you know our son?" Phil's mother asked as she reached out and held Branch's hand, as if giving this strange man some compassion for what he had to go through each day.

"Your son 'it…'" Branch started as Lao interrupted to finish the sentence.

"Phil was hitting the gym Branch owns," Lao snuck in as he looked over at Branch with a pair of cruel eyes.

"But he also 'it…'" Branch said before Lao brushed aside his statement.

"Yes, the other night when Phil hit the deer," Lao said taking over the conversation. "Branch was there to help us," he said eyeing the crippled man with coercion to shut his mouth and leave. "Don't you think it's time to leave, Branch?"

"But he wasn't there when Phil hit the deer," Smyrna spoke up confused. "You were there too, Lao," she said point blank. "This guy wasn't around to help us."

"Oh, that's right," Lao responded, feeling the pressure on both sides as his story of lies was sinking quicker into a sudden phantom of quicksand.

"Then what?" Thya asked as she walked up from behind, catching Lao by surprise. "What else did Phil hit, Branch?"

Branch looked around the circle and swallowed. He eyed Lao as if telling him he couldn't hurt him anymore than they had already hurt him.

As Branch said the word, Lao felt the air leave the place as if Branch took a needle to a balloon. He felt the pop in Phil's parents' eyes. He saw the explosion as dread covered Smyrna's face. He heard the gasp from Thya's lips as she quickly walked over and wrapped her arm about Smyrna for support.

He didn't know one paltry word could cause so much backlash and unresolved problems.

"Me," Branch said with a trembling lip as a tear trickled down his cheek. "Your son 'it me."

"Our son?" Phil's father asked, almost convulsing at the idea that his son had caused the mangling of the man before him.

Branch nodded his head as he looked at Lao.

"Dey all did," Branch said with a downcast look.

"No," Smyrna said in shock as her memory refused to align with Branch's claim. "It was a deer," she claimed. "I saw it. He hit a deer."

Branch looked over at her, shaking his head no.

"He tot he 'it a deer," Branch said through a fragile emotional breath. "But it wuz me."

Thya erupted in a tearful scream as she looked over at the crippled man, probably remembering the events of the night. Lao watched as she looked him up and down probably remembering how Phil had taken his eyes off the road right before he'd collided with something.

"How'd you survive?" Phil's mother asked as her cries unhinged her callousness. "Why aren't you still in the hospital?"

Branch shrugged his shoulder. "A iricle?"

A miracle?

Lao looked over at Branch and wanted to deck the man for causing so much pain for his friends. Pain they didn't have to endure.

"You knew?" Thya looked over at Lao as her eyes switched from grieving to fury.

"What?" Lao balked in shock at the audacity of her statement.

167

"You went to Branch's house where Phil died, so you knew what really happened?"

Thya's questions were overlooked as another set of pieces were falling into place.

"You killed my son!" Phil's father stated with anger quickly erasing the memory of tears a second ago.

"No," Branch said unfazed. "But I onted to."

But I wanted to.

Lao felt a chill drifting into the funeral home. He knew it wasn't Branch's confession that caused the frigidness. It was something much worse.

He turned around and saw a shadow moving closer from the door until it was inches away from his heel. A faint whistle sounded as he suddenly felt frozen in place. His eyes looked over at Branch who had a devilish smile on his face.

"Get out of here!" Phil's father exclaimed as he walked to the door to get the funeral home director.

Phil's mother clutched her heart, reaching out for someone to catch her.

"Jessica!" Phil's father shouted, running back to his wife who was lying on the ground. Thya and Smyrna were leaning over the dying woman, screaming for anyone to help as Jessica started gurgling her last bit of damp air in her lungs.

"Lao!" Thya screamed, looking up at him with pleading eyes. "Go get help!"

But Lao couldn't move. He couldn't do anything but watch and wait for Phil's mother to pass from this life.

"I got it," Branch spit out, turning to hobble away to the door.

Lao's heart dropped, knowing once again it was his angel of death doing this. Branch was free to move about freely.

Branch didn't have to watch Phil's mother die.

"What's going on?" Phil's father screamed, stroking his wife's cheek, his tears landing on her forehead.

Jessica's body tensed up, and her neck strained as all the blood vessels showed through her pale skin. She twisted and convulsed as the angel of death leaned down reaching between Phil's father and Thya. He pointed his long skinny finger an inch from Jessica's forehead and stopped.

It raised its head to look Lao in the face. The emptiness inside the robe filled Lao.

Just do it! Lao pleaded inside his head. *Just kill her!*

"Jessica!" Phil's father cried out, trying in vain to control his wife's abnormal twitches. Her body twisted and bent. She moaned in pain as if begging for death.

Please. Lao begged, watching his friends trying to hold down her arms and legs.

The whistler blew one loud note and ended her suffering by touching Jessica's forehead as it continued to look into Lao's empty eyes.

Lao suddenly felt free as the darkness vanished and the frigidness evaporated like a sizzling summer morning. He walked over and touched Thya's shoulder who looked up unapologetically.

"You did it again," she said through clenched teeth. "You just watched her die like everyone else."

"I…uh…" Lao tried to say, but he couldn't think of anything to say as a wall of emotions surged with full force at his breaking heart. The angel of death reappeared as Lao's heart plummeted. It reached out its bony finger toward Thya's forehead.

No! Stop!

But once again, Lao couldn't speak or move.

CHAPTER 64

Lao watched in agony as the surrounding faces stared in horror. Their mouths gaped open in shock.

"Say something, Lao!" Thya snapped as Smyrna dug her face into the crevice of her friend's arm.

The angel of death stopped and turned its head as it waited for Lao's response.

Lao's eyes darted around the group that watched his actions with mournful expressions. The angel of death looked intently into Lao's eyes, and he looked into the hollowness behind the mask.

He felt like he was falling into the darkness, when suddenly jolted back to reality and the angel of death was gone.

Lao looked around for support, but all he saw were looks of uncertainty and betrayal. He turned and ran out the door; he didn't want to stick around them much longer. He loved Thya, but in the last few days their relationship had quickly come loose for reasons beyond his control.

He wanted nothing more than to tell her the truth. Tell her everything. Tell her all his deepest, darkest secrets so they could run off together and live happily ever after until she died in his arms at the ripe old age of ninety. That was his wish.

But wishes don't come true.

He was stuck in the compromising position of keeping silent or watching untimely deaths.

Lao ran as soon as he reached the outside. He wanted to flee the looks he was receiving. He wanted to disappear from existence so he couldn't hurt anyone ever again. He wanted to exact revenge because he knew in his core the reason for Phil's mother's death.

Branch.

Branch had ensued the group into discord. He was the one to awaken the anger and guilt of looking at the man Phil hit Halloween night. He was the one to accuse the dead of a crime he couldn't defend. Phil's mother's optimism crashed like Phil into Branch's side.

She may not have been physically blindsided, but she was emotionally. She died thinking her son fled the scene of a crime. She tasted death thinking her son was killed by Branch. Her last thought was probably seeing her life as a failure for raising a son like Phil.

Those thoughts were wreaking havoc on Lao's mind. He didn't want to dwell on the negativity and let the angel of death feast upon his thoughts of condemnation. He didn't want to see the creature anymore.

So he continued to run through the city with one place in mind. He didn't know what he was going to do, but he knew he had to try something. If he didn't, things were going to get worse faster than he could control.

He remembered the look on Phil's father's face. The look on Branch's face.

He knew both were capable of unending harm and damage.

That scared him the most—the unknown factor of the entire mess he'd stumbled upon that Halloween night when they walked away from the dying deer.

Lao shook his head wondering how many other people had been put in similar situations.

He stopped running at that thought. All the corruption in the world. All the scandals. All the revengeful workplace shootings.

What if all of those have a common thread?

What if immortals are the reason for the evil in the world?

He now understood immortality would not be all fun and games. It was a living nightmare he would never wake from.

CHAPTER 65

Lao beat on Branch's backdoor with enough force to cause the glass to rattle in its place. He didn't care if it shattered and broke into a million pieces.

Branch had caused so much more damage.

"Branch!" Lao shouted looking down his driveway making sure no one was watching him. That was the fortunate thing about someone living on the outskirts of the city; neighbors were nowhere to be found.

"What you want?" Branch growled from behind the glass door as he reached up and fumbled with the deadbolt.

It's not locked, Lao thought as he quickly pulled open the screen door and gripped the doorknob, forcing himself into the house.

"Get out!" Branch hissed as he backed away from the door looking behind him on the kitchen counter for something to use to defend himself. He grabbed a pair of scissors with his twisted hand, fumbling the handle with his broken fingers.

"We need to talk, man!" Lao said holding his hands up.

Branch lurched forward, swinging the scissors at Lao, who dodged the twitching man. Branch refocused and tried again, launching himself in Lao's direction.

Lao grabbed Branch's shoulder using the oncoming force against him and pivoted him into the wall. Branch stabbed the wall as pieces of paint and drywall fell to the ground.

"Why did you do that?" Lao fumed. "Phil's dead! Why did you do that to his parents?"

"Becuz!" he spit out as he readjusted his stance and found his balance again.

"You didn't have to do that, Branch! You didn't!" Lao growled in return. "Phil didn't purposely hit you. We both got out and thought it was a deer. If we thought we had hit someone, don't you think we would have stopped?"

"I don't care!" he hissed as he held the scissors in front of him, pointing them in Lao's direction. "Dey deserved it!"

"His parents didn't deserve anything you did today!" Lao took a wrestling stance with bent knees and spread arms. "You're just mad you didn't die and you have to deal with this!"

"He 'it me an left me ta die!"

"I left you too, but I'm telling you, I didn't mean it. I'm sorry, Branch! But you went too far!" Lao watched Branch turn into a deranged animal looking for anyone to hurt. "What are you going to do when the cops come? You basically told them you wanted to kill Phil. The cops are going to start investigating and it doesn't look good, Branch. You can't tell them the truth or people will start dying at your feet and then they will start getting really suspicious of you."

Branch didn't care about the question Lao asked or his train of thought.

Lao watched the look in Branch's eyes as it radiated pure hatred. He knew Branch would never let go of this.

Never.

Branch launched forward, but Lao sidestepped him, throwing him into the counter. Branch's arms bent into his body, leaving the scissors nowhere else to go since his crooked fingers couldn't drop them.

"Branch!" Lao said in shock. "I'm sorry, I'm so sorry," he bellowed as Branch looked down slowly turning to show the blue handles protruding out of his stomach.

Lao watched in horror as Branch pulled out the clean pair of scissors with no blood on the edges. They looked at one another in puzzlement as Branch lifted his shirt exposing a tan, rippling midsection with a tear in the middle where the scissors had just been.

CHAPTER 66

Branch dropped the scissors on the floor when he saw they were useless. He rubbed his stomach like he had done many times before, feeling his six-pack abs, but this time he was more intrigued with poking at his new hole. He looked up at Lao as his face showed a thousand different emotions surging with no outlet.

Branch erupted in rage as he spewed out a gut-wrenching groan shaking the glasses in the cabinet. He stomped his feet and looked at Lao as if he once again was the only enemy he had.

"Branch!" Lao said holding up his hands to show a solidarity, but Branch wasn't looking for a pact. He was looking for revenge.

"I can't even kill you!" he groaned in horror. "I can't even kill you!" he kept screaming at the top of his lungs.

"Sorry," Lao said standing his guard. "Nope, we are immortal now." He glanced down at the scissors on the floor. "But I didn't know that would happen."

"Dey told us we couldn't get hurt," Branch commented as he formed a fist.

"Yeah, I guess they did," Lao said nonchalantly. "Not that I believed them because I still don't know who to believe, but I guess they didn't lie about that."

Branch suddenly pounced forward, pushing Lao back and slamming his head into the wall.

It shocked Lao that the crash didn't hurt. He felt the pressure of hitting something, but no pain.

The two men wrestled on the ground before Lao pinned Branch to the floor. He maneuvered Branch around so his face was kissing the linoleum.

"You have to stop!" Lao said, pressing Branch to the ground.

"Never!" Branch grimaced as he twisted his neck to spit on Branch's shoes.

"Dude!" Lao yelled. "You're never going to stop?"

"Never!" Branch screamed at the stop of his lungs as he tried to turn onto his back to grab Lao.

"What are you trying to do?" Lao shouted. "You can't hurt me. I can't hurt you. What are you trying to do?"

"I want you gone!" Branch groaned, drool dripping down his chin in uncontrolled rage.

"You want me gone?" Lao laughed. "I told you, you can't kill me."

"I will get you one day!"

"You know that is impossible."

"I dank I know of a way," he smiled as he looked to his living room.

"Why are you smiling?" Lao followed where Branch was looking. Branch tensed when he saw Lao discovered his intention. "Would you really do that?"

Branch didn't say a word.

"Really?" Lao said in heated thought. "You were going to do that?"

Branch remained silent.

"Look me in the eye and tell me the truth." Lao leaned down to Branch's face with his knee still on his back. Branch closed his eyes. "Look at me!" Lao screamed, opening Branch's eyelids with his fingers.

Branch just smiled as their eyes connected.

"I dank its time for you ta leave."

Lao looked over at the closed cellar door and then back at Branch.

Lao shook his head and grabbed the pair of scissors on the floor behind him. Lao held Branch's hand down, stabbing the scissors through his hand, pinning his arm to the floor.

Branch didn't feel a thing, except the pressure on his back releasing as Lao jumped off of him.

CHAPTER 67

Lao ran over to the cellar door and opened the latch, swinging it freely to hit the wall behind it. He looked down into the darkness once again but couldn't see the bottom.

"Branch, if I can't trust you, I got to do this!" Lao yelled as he ran back to Branch lying on the ground. Branch had removed the scissors from his hand, but he was still trying to get up off the floor. He looked like a helpless turtle rolling on its broken shell.

"Peaze, no!" Branch cried as Lao grabbed Branch's feet and started dragging him on the floor through the living room.

"Why, Branch?" Lao moaned. "You were going to do it to me, weren't you?"

"I…I…I," Branch stuttered in fear as his hands were scraping the floor, trying to dig his nails into the flooring or grab onto the furniture as he passed.

"You're making me do this, Branch!" Lao hissed. "I don't want to, but if it's between you or me…" Lao stopped as Branch clung onto one of his couch's legs. "It's going to be you."

"No, Lao!" he cried as Lao threw Branch's legs down to the ground and walked toward his hands. Lao uncurled Branch's fingers from around the furniture leg and gripped his wrist. He lifted his upper torso and started pulling him again.

"This is all your doing!" Lao said as he slowly made his way to the cellar door. He laid Branch beside the opening, positioning his head over the darkness.

"Peaze Lao!" he cried. "I pomise, I won't do it ta you!"

"Promise?" Lao asked as he stepped on Branch's back. "Because if you try, I will hurt you!"

Branch looked up with a sinister smile. "How?"

"I don't know how, but I will get even if you ever try this again, Branch."

Lao took his foot off of Branch's back and lifted his torso away from the hole in the living room floor, spinning him around.

The two looked at each other with a new strange connection. They knew they could never trust one another again.

That fear got the best of Lao.

He kicked Branch in the face and watched as his body fell backwards into the dark hole.

Lao peered over the opening as he heard Branch's feeble cries. He couldn't see Branch's body on the bottom, but he knew there wasn't any way he was going to climb out of the hole.

Well almost.

He looked at the shabby ladder and touched the wood. He felt it move as if it wasn't even attached. It was just a ladder along the wall.

"Lao!" Branch yelled, but Lao ignored his cries.

Lao gripped the ladder and started pulling up. He groaned at the heaviness of lifting a wooden ladder, but he kept pulling.

"No!" Branch moaned as Lao continued to pull.

Lao had seen nothing like it. He pulled up a ten-foot ladder only to find a rope tying another ladder to the last rung. He kept pulling, ignoring Branch as he pulled out another ten-foot ladder. Once again there was a yellow rope tying another ladder to it. He pulled again until he reached the end of the last one.

Lao fell back looking behind him and saw three ten-foot ladders.

A crippled Branch with probably more broken bones was thirty feet below in complete darkness with no ladder.

"You shouldn't have messed with me, Branch," Lao said closing the cellar door.

He sat on the door and leaned his head down toward the crack, listening for Branch. But all he could hear was a faint muffled yell.

"Lao! Elp! Lao!"

Lao looked around the living room and saw a rug near the front door. He considered moving it but thought of something better.

He grabbed the couch and skidded it across the floor, positioning it over the cellar entrance. He laid on the leather and closed his eyes. He listened for Branch, but it was silent.

Perfectly silent.

As if Branch had left town because he was afraid the cops were on their way.

Yeah, that's what happened. Branch left town.

CHAPTER 68

Lao went through Branch's things and took his keys to get back into the house later when the cops wouldn't be investigating the scene.

He casually walked back to his apartment and laid low the rest of the day. He tried texting Thya, but she wasn't responding. She seemed to be distancing herself from Lao, and he really couldn't blame her. To be perfectly honest, her skills of breaking down the truth were uncanny.

The sun faded over the horizon as Lao's mother returned home from work. He heard her warm up some leftovers while he stayed cooped up in his bedroom, staring out his window and watching the day pass by.

He had a sickening feeling there would be many more days like this one in his unending future. He wondered how many times he would have to move to a new city, pick up a new identity, and hit the reboot button. He definitely couldn't live in Sardis the rest of his existence because even the Hollywood types with their plastic surgery age a little. He didn't know how he would convince his high school alum at their fiftieth high school reunion why he still looked sixteen.

Lao did a few hundred push-ups, stopping periodically to check his phone. There were still no new texts. It was as if the world had forgotten him, or wanted him to disappear. He didn't find enjoyment in trolling through the internet or liking friends' photos on Instagram anymore. It was just another reminder they were normal, and he was anything but.

He watched the night pass by like the sky was an hourglass of painted sand. The yellowing sky dissolved into an indigo blue as if a painter were smearing the colors on his palette, creating a breathtaking new color by adding a blotch of orange and a dollop of blue, a touch of red and a drop of black. The sky swirled into a symphony of colors, changing by the minute like the passionate tempo of Tchaikovsky's *Swan Lake*.

Lao blinked his eyes, and suddenly it was two in the morning. The brilliant blue autumn sky had morphed into a midnight black chilly night. A few stars were scattered overhead as the moon was cycling through its stage showing a little less than the night before.

 Exiting his bedroom, he quietly left the apartment building and found solitude in the driver's seat of his mother's vehicle. He made his way to the same farm as before, but this time it was different.

Branch's car wasn't parked in the same spot it had been. Lao wondered if anyone would miss Branch's slurred speech.

But he was pretty sure if given the choice, the group would have preferred Lao to be at the bottom of the cellar. Not Branch.

CHAPTER 69

Lao mingled around the barn, pretending like he hadn't shoved one of their members down a thirty-foot cellar with no way of escaping.

He tried to fake smile and partake in idle chit-chat, but he felt the judgmental glances. His guilt got the better of him as he theorized that they all knew what happened to Branch and someone had rescued him. Every time he heard the six knocks, his head would dart to the door, expecting to see Branch limp into the meeting circle.

But every time it was someone else, his stomach loosened the knot it had been tightening since the afternoon.

"Heard about your friend's mom," Walter said strutting up in his green robe. "It's a shame it hasn't let up on you yet." Walter stopped and turned his back to the rest of the room, giving his undivided attention to Lao. "I think you hold the record for most deaths in a week."

Lao didn't respond, but his face twitched with the awareness that his chain of deaths was evident to Walter. If they were evident to Walter, then they were most likely known by the rest of the people in the room.

"Um, Walter," Lao said softly.

"Yeah," he answered scanning the group for anyone new.

"If you want to leave the group, can you?"

"Leave? Sure." Walter shrugged. "There are more people in Sardis like us than you would think."

"Really?" Lao stood shocked. "Why don't they come?"

"Why did you ask if people can leave? People leave for various reasons. Some get tired of the same ol' thing each night; some want to pretend like they are not immortal; but mostly, people leave because they move on to new places."

"How many places have you lived in over the years?"

"Oh, jeez," Walter broadly smiled as he mentally counted. "I would say six."

"Huh."

"What?" Walter responded with a puzzled look.

"I just assumed it would be more."

"Just wait. It's not easy to pick up everything and start over and leave everyone you know and love behind," as he walked away.

"I bet it's not," Lao said with a sunken gaze.

"But I heard," Walter said stopping and turning back, whispering in Lao's ear. "Branch has already left."

"How do you know?" Lao asked in assured disbelief.

"Well, wouldn't you skip out of town if you basically admitted to killing a guy?" Walter asked, shaking his head. "Not his smartest move." Walter looked over at Lao and grinned wickedly. "When your friend hit him," he stopped as he watched Lao's eyes widen in fear, "well, it must have messed him up in the head too."

Lao stood motionless. The truth was coming out about Branch and he probably told everyone in the room how he had died. That it was Lao's fault for his dying alone.

"But cheer up, man," Walter said with glee. "You don't have to look at the man you messed up anymore," he said gripping his shoulder like a dear friend. "I bet that makes you feel much better. It would me."

Lao didn't respond as Walter walked away. The words sunk into his mushy brain, saturating the guilt-ridden part of the lobe. Lao realized he had a decision to make, and he had to make it fast.

Everyone in this group knew Branch's condition was partly, if not all, his fault. He had always heard the saying the truth will set you free, but sometimes the truth is told with a few additional lies to help with the freeing process.

Branch was gone. Branch was gone. Branch was gone, he repeated to himself.

Technically, it wasn't a lie.

Branch was long gone. He just wasn't far away.

CHAPTER 70

Lao stood in the same spot under the hayloft for forty-five minutes, staking out the place as if he was observing some wild creatures in their natural habitat. He felt like that description fit this social setting—wild creatures.

He watched as a few of the key leaders socialized and mingled around the room like it was an awkward office Christmas party. Lao studied Enoch with the way his green robe swayed over the dirty floor, never touching the ground but hovering constantly two inches above the surface. Enoch glanced at Lao occasionally, but it wasn't a forced look, more like a casual survey of the room. He searched for Benjamin, but he didn't see him in the mass of green robes.

Judah remained fixed between two unfamiliar people that stood like Greek columns, tall and unshakable. Judah would whisper in each of their ears, but they would never move, except to nod their heads. Lao watched mesmerized as if his two accomplices were more like bodyguards.

But why would an immortal need a bodyguard?

Of course, Branch had needed one.

He wondered if there were saboteurs within this room. He didn't want to consider himself one, but he knew a week ago he would never have considered sending someone falling thirty feet into an abandoned well. In just a matter of a few days, a lot had changed in this world.

He watched, making up stories about the various people in the room. He wondered how many of these people had helped end someone else's life in an act of revenge? He wondered if affairs had happened, or if one member had killed another's spouse for cheating. There was an endless possibility for revengeful killings. He didn't want to continue on this thought journey, but he knew he had trekked down this path already for real.

If he tossed Branch down a well, he was capable of anything, and that thought terrified him.

Lao continued to drift off into his imaginary world of what-ifs and possibilities when he felt a tap on his shoulder. He jumped like a jittery, guilty child caught with its hand where it didn't belong.

"I warned you," he heard a voice say as he looked at the pair of beady eyes that were aged with twenty lifetimes of stories.

Lao didn't know what to say. He didn't know if Elijah was threatening him or if it was a friendly reminder of the rules announced on his first night.

But Lao didn't think it was either of those. He felt like a little kid being slapped by an adult for giving a foolish look.

"Did you hear me, Lao?" Elijah asked, this time looking a little more forceful.

"Yeah," Lao said shrugging his shoulders. "But I don't believe Judah heard you. Do you want to say it a little louder for him?"

Elijah turned around and saw the lurking eyes of Judah across the room.

"If you knew any better, you would stay away from him," Elijah said condescendingly.

"You know my generation," he smiled wickedly, "we don't always listen."

"Oh, you listen," Elijah said as he turned back to face Lao. "I bet you've heard more than you want me to believe."

Lao shook his head unfazed. "No, I'd tell you what I heard if you really wanted to know," he said coolly as he took off his robe. "But your generation is the one that rarely listens."

"What do you mean?" Elijah eyed sadistically, cocking his head sideways.

"Oh, I think you know," Lao winked. "I think you know better than anyone here."

Lao walked away as Elijah yelled something, trying to get Lao's attention. But true to what the older man already believed, he pretended like he didn't hear.

Lao just didn't care anymore. He was done with caring.

CHAPTER 71

Lao returned home before dawn welcomed the day with an autumn gold morning sun. He quietly entered the darkened apartment and flipped on the television. Light radiated from the screen, but it didn't travel very far. The room remained strangely dark as if someone was telling the light to not pass by an imaginary line.

He looked around the room and noticed a dark haze along the ceiling. It hung like Spanish moss on the trees on southern plantations. He turned up the volume on the television as a whistling sound came through the speakers.

He watched the television flicker as if flipping channels on its own until it stopped on an image of a woman sleeping in a bedroom. It was dark, but it was being recorded with a night vision camera as a green glow shone on the sleeping teenager.

Lao jumped to the television screen, pressing his hands onto the glass as if touching the cheeks of the sleeping Thya.

She looked lifeless.

He grabbed his phone and quickly sent her a text. He watched on the screen as her cell phone sprung to life on her nightstand, but she didn't move. She didn't even flinch at the text alert.

"Thya," he groaned in agony. "Please, Thya. Please." He moaned a desperate plea as he called her phone. He watched the device on the screen vibrate, sliding around on the wooden surface. "Come on," he yearned as he watched with terrified eyes as she remained motionless. Her phone went to her voicemail as he croaked her name. "Thya, please call me."

He ended the call and threw the phone across the room. He screamed out, not caring if he woke his mom or neighbors.

His eyes watched the television as a hint of adrenaline coursed through his being. Thya moved slightly as she let out a long breath.

He smiled, relieved as the darkness on the living room ceiling spread down the hallway.

He watched it spawn like a giant spider crafting a web overhead. Suddenly, the television changed scenes. It was another night vision image with a soft neon green glow shining on the bedroom fixtures. The camera zoomed in on the sleeping individual in a large queen bed. He couldn't see the face, but the person was lying on top of their covers in a pair of scrub-looking pajamas.

The camera panned out from the sleeping individual, showing the typical bedroom with a bed, a nightstand, a flat screen television mounted on the wall, and a closet door wide open. The television showed the dark walls that seemed black as it quickly jerked to the other side of the room, landing on a picture hanging on the wall.

Lao thought he saw the whistler for a brief second with its hauntingly glowing face. He leaned closer to the television and watched as the camera slowly zoomed in, bringing the picture into focus.

Suddenly, the various pieces in the bedroom made sense. The flat screen television hung over a sideways power outlet, the cluttered nightstand with an empty wine bottle and four opened pill bottles, the individual wearing scrubs like pajamas.

Lao tried to call out, but he froze. He was glued to the television as if watching his favorite sitcom. The camera continued to zoom in on the family portrait on the wall as tears filled his eyes. His family wasn't perfect, but it was all he had.

The camera quickly zoomed out and over, showing Lao the sleeping woman's face. She looked dead with her blonde hair covering her face, as some ends were draping into her open mouth. The woman shook. Her mouth foamed like she had swallowed some dishwashing liquid.

Lao wanted to close his eyes. He wanted to turn his head. He wanted to do anything to make the show end.

But he knew it wasn't going to.

He had made the angel ruthless with his cunning schemes this afternoon.

The angel hovered over the convulsing woman, trembling like she had hypothermia. But Lao knew it wasn't from the cold as he heard the apartment's furnace humming, blowing out heat.

The whistler shrieked, and Lao's ears felt like they would bleed from the high-pitched sound echoing through the apartment. It sounded like it was coming from all directions.

And technically, it was.

The angel stretched out its bony finger and danced over the woman's forehead, ever so gently twirling its fingers as if conducting a symphony.

Lao watched in agonizing pain, hoping the finger wouldn't touch her head. He longed for his frozenness to conclude, so he could run and rescue his mother.

But his wish didn't come true. It was as if the whistler knew Lao's thoughts.

The angel looked over into the camera and touched her forehead.

"No!"

CHAPTER 72

Lao ran into the deadly room, finding the scene he'd just witnessed on the television screen. His mother looked peaceful after a decade of hard living and low standards. Her blonde-auburn hair was damp as it stuck to her forehead from the nighttime sweat and the handful of pills she'd swallowed with a bottle of wine.

He walked around the bed, still in the dark, picking up the empty prescription bottles. He shook his head knowing this was her own doing. She wasn't on any medication. She had stolen these from the hospital earlier today as each bottle had a different patient name on it.

"Why did you do this?" he muttered under his stolen breath. "Why did you have to kill yourself?"

He put down the containers and lifted the empty bottle of wine. A piece of paper stuck to the green glass bottom as he tried to smell the aroma of the grapes. But he couldn't smell anything. That sense was dead as well.

He pulled off the sticky sheet of paper with a red crusty ring in the middle. Unfolding it, he found a neatly written letter.

Lao,

I could say I wish I was a better mother to you. But the sad truth is I really don't care. It's a hard world out there and I wish I could say that having you by my side made me want to live, but that's not the truth. Seeing you each day made me want to die a little more. Good mothers aren't supposed to say things like that, but I think you know that I wasn't a good mother. I tried to stick it out, but sticking it out just to wake up to another wasted day isn't the life I want to live. I wish I had something better to say, but good luck out there. You're going to need it.

Oh, and don't bother calling your grandmother. She died. I didn't want to put her through a suicide call, so I've been waiting for this day for a while. I got the call this afternoon and knew this was the time. If you find me breathing, don't call the cops or paramedics. Be a good son and just let me die.

He looked down at the letter and didn't know what to feel. Hurt, sadness, betrayal, rejection—a hodgepodge of what he was supposed to be feeling.

But he wasn't feeling anything.

He was just trying to be a good son.

He sat down on the bed making sure not to sit on her ankle and looked at the portrait hanging on the wall. It was a picture of him, his mother, and grandmother taken shortly after his father had walked out of their lives. He stood up and gazed at his mother's face. He had never noticed this on the image before.

He looked at his grandmother's and his faces and then once again at his mother's. He wished he could see what his mother was looking at in the photograph. He and his grandmother were looking straight ahead toward the camera, but his mother had been looking slightly to the left. She had a smile on her face, but it wasn't for the picture.

She was probably already counting down to this day, he thought as he looked at the depressing family portrait.

Was my whole life a lie? he asked himself as he looked into the glass and saw his tormented reflection.

It has been this entire week. And it will be for many more years to come.

CHAPTER 73

The police came to the apartment and walked through their procedures for a suicide. Lao sat on the couch as a dozen strange men and women walked through the living room to his mother's bedroom like it was a come-and-go birthday party. Most of the attendees didn't acknowledge Lao but kept their eyes to the ground, doing their due diligence.

The medical examiner zipped up the body in the black plastic bag and rolled the gurney down the narrow hallway. Lao watched as they bumped the walls with the metal edges, causing scuff marks and gashes where white paint had been a few minutes before.

The three-ring circus finally had its last act as the remaining police officer exited the apartment. He handed Lao a card for child services and a counselor he would recommend.

Lao nodded his head and thanked the officer for his service.

He stood behind the closed door, leaning his back against the flimsy white oak waiting for the police officer's combat boots to die away down the stairs.

He didn't know what to think.

He didn't know what to do.

He was alone.

He closed his eyes and took a deep breath out of habit. He wanted to wake himself up from this cruel, demented dream. He wanted to free himself from the irrational thought process of being an immortal. He wanted to rewind the week to Halloween night.

He pulled out his phone and called his grandmother. He wondered if his mother was correct or if she was already drunk when she wrote the disheartening letter.

But the call went to voicemail, and he couldn't leave a message because the mailbox was full. He ended the call believing people were probably calling to see if she was really dead.

Just like he had.

He leaned against the door and didn't know what to feel. He was numb, just like he had been for the last few days, wishing he could feel something. Anything. But he couldn't. He was in a floating state of existence where his feelings and emotions didn't matter. They were nonexistent.

A glimmer of twisted hope shone through the darkness as he felt a chill in the air.

His guest had returned.

"There's no one else here, so you might as well just leave," he said to the angel.

The angel stood in the middle of the kitchen and watched Lao in intrigue.

"You will not break me," Lao said with a sinister smile. "You can try, but you better just move on." He shrugged his shoulders. "I have nothing left to care about."

The angel shook its head no as he raised his arm up, extending it forward as his finger pointed toward Lao's face.

Lao didn't fall for the intimidation as the angel continued to stand pointing in his direction.

A faint whistle started grow as Lao closed his eyes and smiled.

The whistling got louder and louder as Lao clenched his eyes shut tighter to ignore what was happening. He continued to smile, hoping the angel would back away. But the whistling continued to increase until Lao felt like his insides were trembling.

Lao flinched from the uncomfortable feeling as he felt every bone inside spasm like he was getting shocked with a taser. He tried his best to stay strong, but his eyes finally opened with a look of surrender.

The angel's face shone a red glow that blazed in each of its six holes. The whistling sound had three long punches to the gut as Lao felt something else on his leg.

He looked up and saw the angel's face fuming with fiery red circles as he reached into his pocket. The angel continued to point its long, crooked finger at Lao's face.

"Please, no," Lao moaned as he pulled out his phone.

The angel nodded its head.

"Lao, babe, I just heard the news. I'm so sorry," Thya said in a frantic tone of remorse and forgotten memories of the last few days. "Is it true that your mom killed herself?"

Lao didn't respond. He just stood against the door and felt the words he'd said a minute ago sucker punch him.

I have nothing left to care about.

The angel lingered as if waiting to see the look on Lao's face when he realized that statement wasn't true. He did have something left.

Then he vanished. And the whistling stopped.

CHAPTER 74

The dual funeral for Lao's mother and grandmother came and went. The service was simple as the organ played softly in a room with white flowers and roses. The caskets were open, and they each wore their favorite dress. Or at least the dresses Lao thought were their favorites. He tried his best to remain unemotional. He welcomed mourners, listened to their consolation, and received hugs when arms were spread wide. He wore the mask of a grieving son and grandson, but on the inside his heart was ice.

He stood alone at the graveside with the two holes in the ground and felt jealous. He was envious of their peace of mind as they laid in their caskets six feet away. He'd never been a religious person, but he hoped they were in a better place. If anyone deserved to go to Heaven, he knew his grandmother did. His mother, well, he hoped there wasn't the other place for her sake. Before this week, Heaven was more of an imaginary place that the living clung onto in order to ease some of the stress of the world. And Hell was just a threat to get people to live better. But after seeing the angel of death, he knew there was something bigger than him.

But that something was still questionable.

He stood in the empty cemetery on the outskirts of town staring at the cement crosses and bowing angels. He looked at the stone statues with intrigue. He wished he could hold on to the cold façade, but he knew life would eventually erode through the granite. He knew he would break and more funerals would be in his future.

He wrestled with the thought of picking a side from the various immortal groups with their own beliefs, but each group had its own agenda. He knew that. He also knew if he was a little older, he would be the one using the newbies for his own loved one's personal safety.

But he had to quit jumping back and forth. He couldn't let two people bend his ear and then wonder who was speaking the truth. He saw the fence that separated the groups like the Mason-Dixon Line, and he knew he was going to have to jump to one side and stay there for a while. If for no other reason than to see what would happen for Thya's sake.

He was done relying on the unfounded knowledge of the few who easily give their opinions.

As he walked away from the two plots, he thought he should feel some comfort in his decision. But he felt remorse for not deciding it a few days before.

He might have saved his mother's life.

The next thought cut him deeper.

He might have saved his grandmother.

CHAPTER 75

A few weeks passed after Lao laid his mother and grandmother to rest. The world kept spinning, but his lifestyle shifted. Thya had melted her iciness and started to speak to him. Lao treaded carefully not to cause any bumps in their reconciliation. After a week, they were laughing and texting like they were before Halloween. Once Thya re-entered Lao's life, Smyrna wasn't that far behind.

Phil's death was hard on Smyrna. She was silent and didn't want to open up for the first week. Two weeks after Phil's death, Smyrna started wearing a black turtleneck every day. Lao didn't ask about her choice of clothing since it was probably something she saw on Instagram as attire for grieving girlfriends. She still didn't talk much and had a constant look of depression on her face. Lao had brought it up multiple times to Thya, but she repeatedly asked him to let her grieve in her own way.

During the third week, Smyrna finally brought up Phil to keep his memory alive. Thya winked at Lao the first time Smyrna said his name at the lunch table, as if saying, "Told ya." Smyrna and Lao found an unlikely bond in their grieving. However, Smyrna's was authentic whereas Lao's was theatric. He tried to keep his emotions intact, especially when he heard a whistle.

He had seen the angel of death a few times over the last few weeks, but it had been rare. Any time he heard a whistle he wouldn't look where the sound was coming from. He pretended like it was just a kid whistling in a hallway somewhere. And the angel had taken no one else from him. He hadn't felt the chill of oncoming death. He hadn't known the feeling of paralysis in his body. He hadn't had to watch death overtake an innocent bystander.

Lao received a small life insurance policy that his mother had through the hospital, but it would not be enough to keep up with his meager standard of living. So he got a job with Walter at Frost's after school.

The pay wasn't quite enough to cover all his expenditures since his apartment rent was almost his total take-home pay for the month.

He considered getting another job when an uncomfortable thought pranced into his brain. He mulled it over. The more he thought about it, the more he felt it was a blessing in disguise. He contacted his landlord and ended the lease on the apartment. He borrowed a truck on a Saturday morning and spent the entire day loading up his belongings with the help of Thya and Smyrna.

"Do you need help unloading this?" Thya asked as they stood behind the truck full of his belongings.

"Nah," he said shrugging his shoulders. "My uncle will help me. They already have a room set up for me," he said hugging Thya for helping him. "I'm probably just going to drop off the things I don't need at a shelter or something next week."

"It's awfully nice of your uncle to allow you to move in."

"Yeah, or I would've had to go into foster care."

"Lucky," Smyrna said. "I didn't know you had any family around here," she said. "I don't remember seeing anyone at the funeral."

Lao nodded. "Uncle on my dad's side."

"Oh," Thya said looking at Smyrna convinced. "That makes sense."

The three parted company, and Lao drove through the quiet city streets to the country. He pulled into a driveway and saw his mother's, now his, vehicle parked by the side door. He got out of the truck and timidly walked up the steps to the side door.

"You can do this," he told himself, building some confidence for the decision he'd made. "It will work."

He pulled out a new key chain with six keys on it and found the right one. He felt the latch unlock before he opened the creaky door.

He entered the darkened home and stood in the entryway as the light from the moon cast his shadow into the living room.

"Uncle Branch," he said softly, "I'm home."

CHAPTER 76

Lao walked slowly into the living room, not turning on any lights. He saw the house was just as he'd left it three weeks ago. The couch was still sitting over the cellar door on the floor. He stepped closer and took a seat on the leather couch. He sat in darkness and heard the peacefulness of living in the country. He didn't hear the banging as the neighbors above him dropped their dumbbells. He didn't hear the adulterated conversations of the neighbors beside him. He didn't hear the puttering of vehicles backfiring in the parking lot.

He laid back and heard nothing.

The peace and quiet brought a soothing relaxation as if being mentally massaged by a million pairs of hands. He closed his eyes and felt at ease, even though he was technically trespassing in the home of a man thirty feet below him.

He opened his eyes as a wicked smile grew on his face at the morbid thought. He had an itch of curiosity that needed to be scratched to crack open the cellar door and look below. He wondered if Branch was lying in the darkness still or if he had finally mustered the strength to stand up on his two legs. He envisioned a hoarse Branch from three weeks of screaming out for help, finally succumbing to the agonizing fact that it was hopeless to waste another breath.

He rose from the couch and took a seat on the floor. He lowered his face and listened with eager anticipation for any sound. Any whimper. Any scraping. Any moaning coming from the darkness below.

All he heard was stillness.

His smile grew wider.

He walked over to the kitchen counter and found a tablet and pen to take down some notes. He needed to figure out how to make his job at Frost's pay for his livelihood. He looked down at the blank piece of paper when something shiny near the door caught his eyes.

He noticed the six keys hanging from the key chain still in the doorknob.

He had two vehicles, when he only needed one.

Sell a vehicle, he wrote.

He knew he could get a few thousand dollars for his mother's car. He realized his utilities could decrease because he didn't need heat since he couldn't feel anything, so that would save him some money. He could lower the temperature to the house to just warm enough to keep the pipes from freezing on wintry nights. His water bill could also decease since he didn't need to drink anything and he could shower at other places, like the school gym.

Gym. He looked over at the key dangling from the key chain. He rushed over to the doorknob and pulled the keys out. He looked at the keys in his hand and then looked around the kitchen and living room. It was a nicely furnished home. He looked out the door and noticed that the vehicle Branch had wasn't too shabby.

He went back to the notepad on the counter and started scribbling his new plan.

Run a gym.

He looked down as he lifted his shirt exposing a tight six-pack. He turned around and looked at his physique that was muscular from years of swimming and conditioning reflected in the glass door. He had never thought of being a personal trainer, but he'd never had to think of providing for himself before. He would keep working at Frost's in the evenings just in case things at the gym imploded, but he actually thought this plan would work out nicely.

He was actually seeing a silver lining from all of his storm clouds in the last month.

CHAPTER 77

Lao locked up Branch's house and pulled away in his mother's vehicle in the dead of night. He hadn't been to the secret society meetings for a couple of weeks because he was still trying to grapple with everything that was going on.

He parked the car and walked the path to where it diverged. He looked up at the old farmhouse and wondered who lived there. It had been a couple of weeks since he'd walked down this path, but the house was still as dark and desolate as it had been a month ago.

He walked through the darkened woods, ignoring the owls and suspicious sounds of unknown critters. He saw the barn and left the lurking shadow of his angel of death that seemed to always wait at the entrance of the woods. He had gotten used to the creature always being around over the last few weeks, almost like an annoying little brother that he could shake off.

He knocked on the barn door six times and the door opened. They welcomed and clothed him in his green robe.

"Lao," Walter said walking up to his co-worker and friend. "What made you come tonight?"

Lao shrugged his shoulders. "I really don't know," he answered confusedly. "I just thought I would."

"Well, I'm glad to see you," Walter said as he walked away to mingle with other people he didn't see daily behind his ice cream counter.

Lao walked through the barn and felt welcomed like it was a family reunion. People who had shunned him before were now smiling and acting friendly.

Lao surveyed the barn looking for Benjamin, but once again, he didn't see him among the hooded figures. Enoch surprised Lao when he approached him with a firm handshake and slightly baffled when

Judith smiled warmly. Even Elijah walked across the room just to say a word to him.

"Lao, how are you doing, son?"

"I'm doing okay," Lao said unsure.

"Well, I am deeply sorry for the loss of your mother and grandmother," he said. "I would have come," he said and stopped and looked around. "But you know."

"Yeah," Lao nodded, "I know."

The two spoke for a few minutes when Elijah immediately stopped and looked past Lao toward the door. Lao turned and saw the doorkeeper cloaking a new arrival with a green robe.

"Come," Elijah said, motioning at Lao. "Follow me."

Lao watched as Elijah walked toward the latest member who arrived and patted her on the back.

"Well, come on, Lao," Elijah said as the new member quickly turned around.

"Lao?"

"Smyrna?"

CHAPTER 78

Lao stood looking at his friend in her green robe. He tried to get a few words out, but he just stuttered single one-word questions.

"When? How? What?"

Smyrna understood his confusion as she was also in shock.

"I'll let you two talk," Elijah said as he patted Lao on the back and gave him a quick wink.

"Um…" Lao said still trying to comprehend what was happening. "When did you die?" he asked, lowering his voice as if asking a secretive question, forgetting they were in the safe confines of the barn. "I mean…Well, you know."

"You first," she said, as if not comfortable enough to answer all the vulnerable questions.

Lao told his story of the night of the séance in the cemetery on Halloween night. How he'd fallen and hit his head on a tombstone and entered this strange loophole.

"It all makes sense now," she said as she listened to him speak. "How you watched Reid, Phil, the waitress, Phil's mom," she stopped and almost started to cry. "Your mom." She started to get emotional and wrapped her feeble arms around his neck. "I'm so sorry, Lao."

"Have you had to experience anything like that yet?" he asked. "Have you watched someone die?"

She nodded her head. "Well, nothing like you," she said carefully. "But most my pets have died."

"Pets?" Lao asked flabbergasted before he quickly apologized.

"It's okay, but my pets are very dear to me."

"I'm sorry, Smyrna."

"I'm sorry for you too. I just don't understand all of this."

"You and me both," he smiled. "It's a messed-up deal we are in."

"If I knew this was going to happen when I killed myself, I wouldn't have done it," she said.

"Wait? What?" Lao asked, deeply saddened. "You killed yourself?"

Smyrna nodded her head as she reached up and pulled her turtleneck down exposing discoloration where something was tightened around her neck. "I hung myself two weeks ago."

"Two weeks ago?" Lao asked in shock. "You know, I thought something was different about you. I remember asking Thya if you were alright, but she told me to let you grieve in your own way." He hit himself on the forehead. "That's why you've been wearing turtlenecks all the time. To hide your wounds."

She nodded her head. "Guilty."

"Oh, Smyrna," Lao said pulling his friend into a warm embrace. "I wish I could have warned you. I wish I could have told you to not do that." He stopped and looked at her solemnly. "If I knew you wanted to die, I wish you would have died when I was around you."

"I know," Smyrna said with a tear rolling down her cheek. "Funny isn't it," she said with a forced laugh. "I wanted to die because I couldn't stand to be away from Phil one second longer, and now..." she stopped and turned her head.

Lao knew exactly what she didn't say.

CHAPTER 79

Lao and Smyrna spoke until sunlight was peeking through the wooden slats of the barn. They parted ways with a look of trust in one another's eyes. Smyrna returned home and Lao headed toward Branch's gym.

He parked behind the building and found the key to unlock the back door. He walked through the dark office and saw a room lit up at the end of the hallway. He heard loud music blaring and the sound of someone grunting.

Lao nodded to the muscular man lifting fifty-pound weights over his head as he watched himself in the mirrors. Branch's gym, Elite Fitness, was open 24 hours a day with gym members getting through the locked front door with a key fob.

"I'm Lao," he said introducing himself. "Branch is going to be away for some time, and he has asked me to watch over the place while he is gone."

"You look a little young, kid," the man said dropping the weights to his side.

"Yeah, but it shouldn't be for long," Lao lied. "Uncle Branch should be back soon."

"Where'd he go?" the man in red jersey shorts and gray t-shirt asked as he stood up to exchange weights.

"You know Branch. He probably found some type of race out West. Knowing him, he's probably biking there," Lao laughed as the man nodded and grunted.

Lao walked around the gym, finding random rags hanging on the equipment and picked them up. If this was now his, he wanted to keep it clean.

"Well, if you need anything, just let me know." Lao walked away with an armful of sweaty, dirty towels.

He dropped the towels beside Branch's desk and started to investigate. He lifted the keyboard and found all of Branch's security passwords and phrases. Within minutes Lao had access to all of Branch's financials. He logged into Branch's bank accounts and saw his house had no mortgage. He even had a decent amount of money in his personal checking and savings accounts. Lao switched over to his business accounts and saw the payday he was hoping to find. Elite Fitness had various loans, but it also seemed to be a fairly stable business with a large influx of members fee deposits each day.

Lao grinned at the turn of events. Yesterday, he was a broke orphan on the verge of having to decide which things in life he would have to say farewell to. Now, he was a financially stable business owner.

CHAPTER 80

The next week was unlike anything Lao had experienced in the last month. He had a friend he could express all of his deepest fears and concerns to. He went to school for a few hours a day and used Elite Fitness as a co-op program allowing him to get school credit. He actually had two jobs that he loved. He could embrace his love for fitness and help those struggling during the day and indulge people's sweet tooths in the evening.

It was a win-win.

He continued to meet with Smyrna each evening at the barn. Every once in a while, they would sneak off and explore the grounds of the farmland under the light from the moon.

The weeks passed and December's winter air rolled into the town of Sardis, but Lao didn't feel the effects. He didn't feel the freezing cold temperature as he sat in his home, but he rarely went home. He was either at school, the gym, the ice cream shop, or the barn. *When you're an immortal, there really isn't much need for a place to rest.*

Lao won the rest of his swim meets, even coming in first place at state, easily beating everyone in the 200-meter freestyle race. His two biggest supporters were there to watch and cheer, Thya and Smyrna.

The three of them had become tighter than ever before. Smyrna had only been a friend to Lao by association of Thya before Halloween. Now, Lao looked at Smyrna like a sister he never had.

See you tonight? Smyrna texted.

Yes, Lao texted back. He looked down at his phone and felt at peace even though he saw the angel of death in the gym's mirror standing beside Lisle running on a treadmill with earbuds in her ears.

Lao hadn't felt fear in the last few weeks. He hadn't seen the angel as anything more than a lurking shadow. But something felt different now.

Lao watched the angel, but he didn't hear the same whistle. It sounded like it was a different octave or a distinct note altogether.

He felt an incredible jolt of cold hit him. His eyes widened as the mirrors started playing tricks with his vision as another angel appeared, looking to be in a different part of the room.

He turned around to see the angel still standing beside Lisle. He turned his head and saw another angel standing in the doorway to the men's locker room.

His ears rang as he heard two different whistles. His head went back and forth, watching the two angels when suddenly he felt his neck freeze. He couldn't turn his head.

He wanted to close his eyes, but he couldn't. His eyes locked onto Lisle jogging carefree on the treadmill. He heard the two angels whistle and it sounded like they were whistling to one another, as if communicating.

The gym had a few other members on bikes and ellipticals, a couple on weight machines. They were all oblivious to the chaos that was about to ensue.

Lao knew something deadly was about to happen.

Branch's angel?

CHAPTER 81

"Hey, Lao," Dirk, a fitness regular, shouted from his weight bench. "Can you spot me?"

"Sure," Lao said without trying to speak. His body eased and he walked over to Dirk who was already lying back ready to lift his weight. He had loaded each side of the bar with 150 pounds.

Lao walked over in shock. It was as if he was a robot. He wasn't controlling his movements. He felt like his arms and legs were floating, like a marionette.

His eyes widened as fear rose exponentially when his body stopped at Dirk's head. He looked forward and he could see the angel standing beside Lisle. To his side he saw another angel stooping down, admiring Dirk's chiseled triceps.

Lao tried to alleviate the fear, to not think about what was about to happen. He tried to change his thoughts to being positive and not afraid.

It didn't work. No matter how much he tried to refocus his attention, his eyes were darting between Dirk and Lisle.

The angel beside Dirk raised up and placed one of his deathly hands on the weighted bar. Dirk started to struggle. His bulging arms twitched. All the air in his lungs squeezed out of his mouth as his teeth clenched, gritting in pain.

"Lao," he tried to say, but it was just a gasp of tired air escaping his mouth.

Lao looked up at the angel whose mask blazed a fiery red glow as it screamed a whistle. The angel pressed all its strength down, forcing the bar closer and closer down.

Dirk's eyes widened as he saw the bar inching closer to his face.

Lao couldn't look away from the man's terrified eyes. Even though Dirk's words couldn't be uttered, he knew what he was trying to say. Lao felt the fear.

Lao had his hands under the bar, but he wasn't able to help lift it. He was following the angel's wicked orders, unable to do anything but just stand there, watching and waiting for the bar to drop.

The angel blew another powerful blow. The whistle flooded Lao's ears like razor blades as its finger inched closer to Dirk's forehead.

Lao didn't want to watch, but he couldn't look away.

Lao's insides cringed at the sight of so much blood. He never wanted to know what the inside of someone's head looked like.

Now he wasn't ever going to forget it.

CHAPTER 47

"Branch!" Lao darted into the garage and saw Phil lying on the ground with his hands and feet tied and a puddle of blood forming under his head. He looked toward the whistling sound and saw a dark shadow lingering in the back corner, ready to take its next victim. Two angels stood against the wall as if deciding who was going to kill Phil.

Phil's eyes widened. His gagged mouth didn't allow him to scream, but his eyes verbalized the terror he was feeling.

"Ut are you doin 'ere?" Branch hissed with disdain.

"Branch, you don't want to do anything stupid. You are not a murderer."

Phil groaned at the word murderer. He rolled around like a fish out of water, inching himself away from the trajectory of Branch's gun barrel.

"Drop the gun, Branch!" But Branch didn't follow his order. He just smiled a wicked half grin.

"He dit this to me."

"It was an accident, Branch," Lao answered. "He didn't mean to do that to you." Lao moved a little closer, thinking if he was within arm's reach he could jump and attack Branch and subdue him without harming Phil.

Lao looked around the garage and saw Branch's riding lawnmower beside his gas containers and oil cans. Everything was meticulously in its place with gardening tools hanging on the wall, displayed in order of size. Larger color-coordinated, green-handled tools were lining the wall with shovels, hoes, rakes, and spades.

Branch was trembling, either from the wear on his body or fearful remorse. He clutched the gun with one hand and lit a cigarette with the other.

CHAPTER 82

Screams erupted in the gym. Dirk's blood oozed out of his broken skull forming an ocean of blood under the weight bench. The red continued to spread over the gray matted floor, ebbing to Lao's sneakers that were already splattered with droplets of blood.

Lao couldn't move. Usually once the angel would leave, he was unfrozen. Members were calling for paramedics as a few of the others circled around Dirk's dead body, taking the bar off of his head and pushing the weights to the side.

Lao looked up, and his stomach fell as one angel was still there beside the running Lisle.

He watched through two mirrors as Lisle's eyes realized a commotion was occurring behind her. She let out a scream when her eyes found the blood and dead body on the weight bench.

"Dirk!" she screamed, forgetting about turning off the treadmill. Her earbuds cord dangled down her neck to her phone placed securely on the treadmill's mount.

Lao watched the cords. He didn't know why his vision was being narrowed to the cords, but he had a sickening feeling that he was about to find out.

He watched as the angel beside Lisle quickly wrapped her dangling cord around the treadmill's heart rate handles.

What can that do? Lao thought.

Lisle turned, still screaming, as she reached to pull the emergency stop latch, but she missed. The treadmill continued its fast pace as she missed her footing.

She tried to catch herself, but her sweaty, slippery hands didn't grasp the handle tightly enough. Her body went down as the angel placed one hand around each of her ears. Her legs went from under her and flew back off the treadmill, but something caught her.

Her earbuds cord tightened, snapping her neck back.

Her eyes went lifeless as the angel released her ears and touched her forehead before it vanished.

Lao moved from his frozen state as he watched the dead Lisle dangle from her eerily secure earbuds. The treadmill continued to spin its powerful wheels, as it quickly tore through her layers of skin. Blood flowed off the treadmill mat forming a red waterfall

"Stop the treadmill!" Lao screamed as someone ran over and hit the button.

It looked unbelievable that a woman was dangling from the cord of her earbuds wrapped around the treadmill handle.

But Lao had learned over the last month that nothing was unbelievable.

Lao ran to get rags to clean up the blood. There wasn't anything he could do for Dirk or Lisle.

Their three years of marriage ended just like their vows had said. Till death do they part.

CHAPTER 83

After questioning everyone in the gym, the police labeled Dirk's and Lisle's deaths as accidents. Very freaky accidents. Lao put a sign on the front door that Elite Fitness would be closed for three days for cleaning. It was supposedly the first time in Elite Fitness history that its doors would remain closed for more than a few hours.

He went to Frost's for his evening shift and mind-numbingly scooped ice cream for four hours. Three a.m. couldn't come quick enough. He had so much he wanted to speak to Smyrna about in the safe confines of the barn. He wished he could trust the other members of the group, but his confidence in their loyalty was still pending. But the crucial question that lingered in his head as he wiped down the counter at Frost's was why there were two angels of death that day.

Has Branch's angel gotten bored being trapped in the well and started following me?

Walter and Lao cleaned up Frost's after the last customer left them with a chocolate crusty table and a measly quarter tip stuck on the surface by a layer of caramel.

"Nice," Walter said sarcastically holding up the gooey coin. "Want to split it?"

"It's all yours if you take out the trash," Lao laughed as he washed the spoon.

"Nah," Walter replied as he flipped the quarter in Lao's direction. "You're the newbie, you get the trash."

They finished their duties and headed out for the evening. Lao went back home to sit and wait. He hoped the silence would bring some clarity to his situation, but the more he thought, the murkier the proverbial crystal ball appeared.

He reclined on the couch over the cellar door just like he did every night. He would close his eyes and wait for any sound that was stirring underneath. After a month of house sitting in Branch's abode, he heard nothing that warranted an uneasy feeling. He actually hoped Branch had somehow ended his existence.

That thought had brought many nights of envious daydreams of finding the loophole out of this place. *If Branch has done it, maybe I could too.*

He had often thought about moving the couch, opening the door, and shining a flashlight down into the darkness to see if Branch had lost his immortality. But the moment Lao would lift the couch an inch, a little dreadful rationale would come into his head. He would place the couch back down and dismiss the thought.

He liked the peacefulness of the room. If Branch knew someone was living in his house, he would most likely start screaming again for help.

The peacefulness would be over.

Lao looked at the clock on the wall.

It was time to leave.

CHAPTER 84

Lao knocked on the barn door six times. He entered the secret society and waited for his one and only true immortal friend to walk through the door.

He ignored everyone in the room and waited for Smyrna. A few people came up to Lao and asked about the commotion at the gym. They never asked where Branch ran off to, but there was an unspoken belief that since he'd admitted to wanting to kill Phil, he ran off to start another life. Some people questioned why Lao had taken over Branch's living arrangement, but the questions drifted away because they all had done that one time or another. The group had never shared that side of their lives, but Lao could tell that they didn't disapprove of his squatting rights. He knew they wished they had done it themselves.

Lao didn't speak much of the tragedies today. He didn't want to go into the details with people he couldn't trust. They didn't deserve the details.

Lao stood along the wall anxiously waiting until his friend stepped through the door.

Lao rushed across the hay-covered floor. "Smyrna."

"Lao, how are you doing?" she asked with an expression of concern.

"Smyrna, we need to talk," he whispered into her ear. She nodded her head. "In thirty minutes behind the farmhouse."

"The farmhouse?" she asked in shock. "Is it safe?"

"Is it safe in here?" he questioned as he walked away to mingle with the others.

That was the question of the ages.

Or at least it was one of the millions he had.

CHAPTER 85

Lao walked up the gravel path to the eerily quiet farmhouse. He had seen the house from afar every time he had visited the barn, except when he sat in its back yard and spoke to Judah.

Lao looked up and noticed linen curtains hanging at every window. He wondered why there wasn't any light shining from a window. Any window. But it was like the owner's abandoned the farmhouse. As if its owners had died and no one cared about it anymore.

Lao found the two chairs that he and Judah sat in, still in the same place as if not a day had gone by. Lao walked past the metal green chairs and stayed closer to the house, lurking in the shadow from the light reflecting from the moon.

Smyrna approached Lao who was leaning against the vinyl siding. "What is this about?" she asked confused. "Why the secrecy?"

Lao shook his head and stared down at his firmly planted feet.

"What is it, Lao?" she asked, moving within inches of his downcast face.

"How many different angels have you seen?"

"Different?" she asked baffled. "If they're different, they all look and sound the same."

Lao knew she had only seen one. He looked up and caught her blank expression.

"I've seen two," he said as he took a deep breath, "at the same time."

"At the same time?" she asked, amazed. "Whose angel did you see?"

"That's it," Lao said with a twisted smile. "They were both using me to finish their kills."

"At the gym?" she gasped.

"Yeah," he said casually. "Two different angels killed today at the gym, and I had to watch both of them."

"But why?"

"I think I have someone's angel following me," he said concerned.

"How?"

"Smyrna, if I knew that, I wouldn't have asked you to come here."

"Why don't you ask them?" she said, pointing toward the unseen barn behind the woods. "They probably know what it means."

Lao shook his head at her naivety. "You're the only one I trust, Smyrna. The only one."

"Why? Why can't you trust them?"

Lao didn't know where to begin with the last two months of trust and deception. It seemed like no matter what he did, he always walked away a little more wounded than before.

He kicked his feet, hitting the side of the house and causing a slight ripple of sound through the quiet.

That breaking of silence caused something to come awake from behind the four walls.

"Do you hear that?" Lao asked as he closed his eyes.

"Hear wh—" she started to ask as Lao shushed her.

"Listen," he mouthed without making a sound.

Lao's ears perked at the sound of a muffled murmuring coming from somewhere inside.

"What is that?" she softly asked as Lao opened his eyes, looking into her unveiled ones. Her eyes sparkled with intrigue as they darted around, trying to discover the starting point for the cries. "It's coming from inside the house."

Lao nodded his head in agreement.

"So," Smyrna said with a new ray of hope, "are we going in or what?"

CHAPTER 86

Lao stepped away from under the farmhouse eaves following Smyrna around the house.

"What are you doing?" Lao asked, lurking like her apprentice.

She didn't stop moving but continued to circle the house. "I'm looking for a way in," she said flatly as she traced her hands around the filthy glass windows, trying to pry a window open.

"I was told to never go in this house." Lao remembered the second night in the barn when Walter gave the warning.

"I was never told that," she said playfully.

"Well, I'm telling you now," he said sternly.

"Who told you?" she asked. "Aren't you the one who said you couldn't trust anyone?"

Suddenly, Lao found himself in another paradox. He looked back over the past few months and still didn't know who to trust. All he knew was his friend was with him now.

"So you're going to break in?"

"What would you suggest?" she questioned turning her head in Lao's direction. "Knock on the door and wait to see what comes to answer?"

"*What?* Don't you mean *who?*"

Smyrna glanced over her shoulder. "You heard what I said."

Lao tried to shake off the chilling thought, but it was going to be hard. He would not easily forget what he just heard Smyrna say in all seriousness.

"Like an animal?" Lao asked, trying to calm his anxiety.

"You can say that." Smyrna continued to walk along the outside of the house, rubbing the siding as she walked. She took a step and they both heard something besides grass underneath her feet. She looked down and tapped her foot.

Lao's eyes widened as it sounded like she was knocking on a front door. Before he could say anything, Smyrna knelt down and started feeling on the ground. She raked her fingers, sweeping away the grass clippings covering the top of the wooden door. They found a metal rod shoved between two handles like a makeshift lock.

"Looks like it's an entrance to go under the house," she said as she looked over at Lao and twisted the rusty rod through the handles until she lifted it to eye level.

Lao didn't know what she wanted him to say, so he said nothing. He was speechless as he cautiously looked behind him.

"I think we're clear," she said stooping down and raising the solid wooden door. The hidden entryway squeaked through its rusted hinges as the door fell to the grass beside it.

The two looked uneasily at one another, as if daring the other to take the first step into the darkness.

"Ladies first," Lao said with a chivalrous grin.

"I'm not a feminist," she snapped back. "I'm an equalist," she smiled as she grabbed Lao's hand, pulling him beside her. "We'll go in at the same time."

Lao didn't worry about his manly demeanor much, and this probably wouldn't be the last time he wouldn't mind being last for a change.

"What are you so scared of?" Smyrna hissed. "It's not like they can hurt us." She rolled her eyes as she stepped down into the stairwell.

That sentiment didn't bode well with Lao. Sure, they couldn't kill him, but they could definitely inflict harm. It may not be physical pain, but psychological pain seemed much more damaging.

Just as he had been doing to Branch.

CHAPTER 87

Lao followed closely behind as Smyrna sank deeper into the darkness. She brushed away cobwebs in her path, raising her cell phone to light the dark passageway. Lao gripped his phone as he swung his arm in all directions, shining the light behind and beside them. The aged wooden beams along the walls looked strong and sturdy. Lao hoped termites hadn't feasted on the hearty logs as he visualized literally being buried alive for eternity.

Smyrna turned her head and placed a finger over his mouth. Lao searched through the silence for any slight sound. Every second that passed allowed him to go further into the void. A void that yearned and moaned, as if welcoming the two new guests or warning them.

"Do you hear that?" Lao whispered as Smyrna stopped and turned around. She reached out her hands and gripped the wooden beams on each side of her. She closed her eyes and breathed in the dust and mold from years of decay.

They listened to the agonizing moan as another sound echoed through the hollow drowning out the weak moan.

"Lao!" Smyrna shouted, her eyes opening at the sound of the slamming doors behind them. "Run!"

Lao turned around, running toward where they'd come in, but now the opening that had cascaded moonlight was closed. The two ran up the steps, pounding their fists on the locked wooden door. They pressed and pushed up as the door cracked, allowing just a sliver of moonlight into their eyes.

"Help!" Lao screamed as Smyrna also started yelling for rescue.

"Let us out!" Smyrna groaned as they continued to push up with their four hands.

Lao raised his head, catching sight of a couple pairs of shoes standing in the distance, as if watching their pleading.

"They're watching us," he whispered into Smyrna's ears whose arms went weak. She looked through the splintered part in the wood and saw a small crowd circling the entrance.

"Who are they?" Smyrna asked as she stepped away from the door.

"It's them," Lao said convincingly, even though Smyrna still didn't understand who *them* was.

Lao stepped down onto the solid ground and dashed up the path they had walked earlier. His fear was becoming balanced by rage.

"There has to be another way out," Lao said as Smyrna followed behind.

"We have our phones," Smyrna said with a wicked grin. "We're not stuck in here."

"But someone is," Lao said sinisterly, looking overhead as the moaning once again came through the floor.

"Ready to find out?" Smyrna asked as she quickly sent a text message.

"What are you doing?" Lao asked as he heard the sound of a text being sent.

"Just playing it safe," she winked. She quickly outpaced Lao, running ahead, turning one corner and then another, swatting cobwebs like she was playing a video game.

She swung her flashlight and found the second set of stairs. She lifted her hand and dropped her phone from her grip in fright. The phone flipped, shining for brief moments like a Ferris wheel of light. She let out a squeal, but it was quickly muffled.

The phone collided with the ground.

The light went out.

CHAPTER 88

"Smyrna!" Lao shouted as he turned the corner and found an empty set of stairs leading up to a locked door.

Lao spun around, shining his light in front of him, pointing the brief glimmer of hope like a pistol. Fear seized him. "Smyrna!" he shouted once again. He looked behind and then up the steps.

He didn't think Smyrna would have run up the steps and left without him. Something didn't feel right. Lao didn't know how to describe it, but something was definitely wrong.

He took a step, putting his weight on the wooden stairs leading up to the house. The step groaned from the weight, as if giving the house a warning that an intruder was present.

He took another step when he heard a scuffle to his side. He turned, shining his light in its direction to see a pair of beady eyes with its mouth covered by a long bony hand.

"Smyrna!" Lao screamed in horror. "You can't!" he stumbled over his tongue that was swelling in his mouth. "You can't hurt her! She's already dead!"

The angel looked down at the trembling Smyrna and then back at Lao. It didn't let go, but clutched its fingers tighter over her mouth.

"Lao!" she moaned, reaching forward for his free hand.

Lao instinctively reached forward and gripped her hand and pulled with all of his might. She didn't budge. Her eyes were clenched shut, her arms were swinging, fighting the creature with her immortal arms.

"Smyrna!" Lao groaned as he pulled to no avail. There was only one thing left to do.

He revved his arm back, aimed for the face, and leaned into the punch. He saw his fist hit the mask. It didn't feel like plastic or metal; rather his fist sunk into the creature like swinging at a cloud of smoke.

He fell forward, falling into the dark robed angel as if it were a hologram. Yet it clung onto Smyrna like it was granite.

"Lao!" she moaned in shock seeing him fall to his knees on the ground. "Get help!" she yelled, breaking through its grip. Lao jumped up and ran up the stairs. He threw open the door and his insides froze instantly.

"Lao! No!" Benjamin screamed. "Run!"

CHAPTER 89

Seven angels encased the standing Benjamin in a shoulder-to-shoulder circle. Each of their necks spun and tilted as they saw a new visitor standing with the door open.

Lao didn't register what was happening but stood frozen in fear. His mouth went dry and his tongue grew numb. He tried to speak, but nothing came out but a gasp.

An angel gripped Benjamin's mouth, sealing it shut with its bony fingers. The man's eyes widened as he squirmed and kicked with all his might.

Lao darted to the left, passing an angel as it turned and stepped away from the circle. The remaining six angels tightened around Benjamin, closing the gap. Benjamin tried to warn the fleeing Lao, but he couldn't.

He ran through the darkened kitchen, tossing a chair behind him, trying to slow the angel down. It didn't. The angel hovered through the flying four legs. Not slowing. Not dodging. Not feeling any effects of the world.

Lao ran through the swinging kitchen door, entering a formal dining room with place settings that seemed fitting for Valentine's Day. He looked back, watching the door swing back and forth. He continued to run, but he longed for the door to hit the angel.

But the angel just moved through the swinging door unscathed, even as the door swung through its body. Lao's feet stumbled, tripping over an area rug, but he overcame the loss of balance. He felt it sliding underneath, like a surfer on a wave. He spread his arms like a man on a high wire and recovered.

Lao ran through the living room to the front door. He gripped the knob, but it didn't budge. He pulled with all his might, but it didn't crack or move. Pounding on the painted glass, he wished his knuckle would break through the pane. But it didn't. He looked quizzically at his bent wrist smashed against the window. He wondered what that would have felt like if he was still alive.

He looked in the glass's reflection and saw the angel lurking behind. He turned and ran away into an adjourning room. His speed was no match for the angel's cunning desire to play cat and mouse.

Lao ran through a sitting room to a seating area in front of a bay window. He picked up a snow globe on the mantle and threw the paperweight at the glass. It collided with the foggy glass like a heart-sickened boy tossing pebbles at his love's window. Lao's heart fell like a jilted lover. The snow globe burst open as water splashed and fell down the unbroken panes. Lao looked in shock as he tried it again, but the snow globe just exploded when it hit the impenetrable glass.

Lao ran through the house, darting the angel for what seemed like hours. He ran up one set of stairs to the second floor and then ran down the other set. He knew he couldn't hide in any closets or under any beds.

All he could do was run.

And run is all he did.

After running in complete darkness repeatedly, he got an idea.

CHAPTER 90

Lao ran up the stairs for the twenty-second time. He rounded the banister and felt something drawing him to a closed door. He had run past it twenty-one times before, but this time something compelled him to turn the knob.

It turned easily as Lao watched the angel glide up the stairs from his peripheral. He threw open the door and basked in a crack of sunlight through a smeared glass window. Lao ran over to the window and pulled the blinds to the side. He rubbed his hand along the windowpane, wiping away the gunk that was blanketing the light away.

His hand squeaked against the newly polished window. He peeked his head through the clean circle and saw a group of seven individuals casting a shadow toward the house from the morning sun. Lao thought he recognized a few of the people, but not all of them.

"Elijah!" Lao screamed at the top of his voice. "Enoch! Judith! Judah!"

He looked down at the huddle of men and women and wondered if they could see him.

They could.

And as they each turned their head his direction, he knew he was being watched.

Lao turned his head and saw the angel moving into the light.

He got up and hunkered closer to the wall, pressing his back against the hardness and inching himself away from the angel. Lao passed another window, grabbed the blinds, and pulled down, causing the flimsy cloth to tumble to the ground and lay like a dirty shirt on Lao's bedroom floor.

Another ray of light shone into the darkened room.

Lao didn't know why, but the light was easing his fear. It was causing his anxiety to subside. He looked out the window and saw the seven individuals. Once again, he screamed the names that he knew.

As he said the names, the angel stopped and twisted its head. Lao jumped, hurdling himself over the bed.

The angel whistled six quick blows. It paused and then whistled another six quick blows. After pausing, it did it once again.

Lao watched as the angel stared out the window.

"Lao!" Benjamin screamed from the floor below. "Lao!"

"Ben!" Lao yelled, following the sound of his screams. He turned to find the closest set of stairs as he stopped.

A group of angels was climbing up the incline.

He slinked back against the wall, turning to run. He ran around the floor, following the hallway to the other stairwell.

"Lao!" Smyrna screamed. "Come on!"

"Smyrna!" Lao shouted as he walked into the darkness, gripping the handrails of the stairs. He got halfway down and stopped.

A group of angels were slowly rising.

Lao turned and ran back. He expected to see a few angels, but they weren't in the hallway. He passed the room he'd been in before, and something strange caught his eye.

"Lao!"

CHAPTER 91

"Come on!" Benjamin shouted from downstairs.

Lao stood in the doorway for a split second, but it felt like an hour. He watched as the angels stood in line in front of the two windows when suddenly, one of their hands pierced through the unbroken glass. It sounded like all the angels blew a whistle, sounding their freedom.

The first angel went through the window, floating with its arms and legs as flat as a board. Then another one went through.

Lao ran toward the stairs and circled the banister. He started taking two steps at a time, running down the stairwell as he saw from the corner of his eye the remaining angels herding into the bedroom.

Waiting to be freed.

Lao reached the ground floor, running toward the screaming Smyrna in the kitchen with Benjamin.

"What's going on?" Lao asked looking around the room in disbelief.

"They're free," Benjamin said with a blank stare.

"You mean *we're* free," Lao said.

"No," Benjamin said shaking his head, "*they're* free."

Smyrna's eyes widened in shock. "Are you saying they captured their angels and put them here?"

Benjamin nodded his head as the three stood in the kitchen, unsure of what to do next.

"Then why were you here?" Lao asked with a confused look.

Benjamin looked around the room, opening various drawers under the cabinet. His eyes were fixated in the search. He opened a drawer with potholders and towels and moved on. He opened another drawer with rolls of plastic wrap and aluminum foil. He pulled a final drawer and smiled like a kid finding a stash of candy.

He picked up a knife and nodded his head for the others to pick one as well.

"I'm in here because I spoke to you," Benjamin said nonchalantly. "Ready to get to work?"

CHAPTER 92

Lao and Smyrna each picked up a sharp, sturdy knife and followed Benjamin out the door and down the steps into the basement.

"What do you mean, 'because I spoke to you?'"

"Your good friend, Judah," Benjamin said snidely as he walked into the darkness, clutching his knife in his hand. "He put me here."

"Because you talked to me?" Lao asked in shock, holding the knife at his side. "Why?"

"Lao, you just don't get it." Benjamin stopped and turned around. "If they distrust you, they will try to get rid of you."

"What good would that do?" Lao asked, still not seeing the rationale in Benjamin's words.

"Think about it, Lao. When was the last time you saw me?"

Lao thought for a few seconds before Benjamin interjected.

"Yeah," he said. "You can't remember because it's been that long."

"How long have you been in here?" Smyrna reacted with a raised voice.

"I'm lucky," Benjamin grinned. "Without you two disobeying orders, I would have been in here much longer. So, I guess I should thank you instead of lecturing."

Benjamin turned and walked faster and further into the darkness as Smyrna stooped down and picked up her phone she had dropped earlier in the night.

"Are you okay?" Lao asked her, helping her up.

"I don't know," she said with a fragile tone. "I was scared to death," she said as she and Lao realized that phrase didn't matter to any of them. "Well, you know what I mean."

Lao nodded as he looked forward and lost sight of Benjamin.

"Where'd you go?" Lao asked as he fumbled around for his phone and turned on the flashlight.

"There's no where we can go," Benjamin said agitatedly up ahead, "until we get through this door."

Benjamin reached the door and started jabbing the knife into the wood.

"Are you trying to stab it to death?" Smyrna asked sarcastically.

"What do you suggest? Because we have to get out of here fast!"

"Fast?" Lao asked. "Why?"

Benjamin continued to stab the door, flaking the wood bit by bit. "Do you not realize what you just let out?"

Lao shook his head and looked over at Smyrna.

"Oh, dimwitted teenagers," Benjamin huffed with a chuckle, shaking his head with disdain. "To be so naïve."

"Hey, dude, we saved your ass," Smyrna scolded with her hands on her hips.

Benjamin stopped and nodded in suppressed agreement. He turned back and continued to stab the wood, holding one hand over his eyes to keep the chips of wood out of them.

"So, what are we naïve about?" Smyrna asked, full of teen attitude.

He didn't stop jabbing, but stabbed harder. "You just let out seven angels that have been locked up for who knows how long," Benjamin said as his speed and strength intensified.

Benjamin made a fist and punched up into the center of the door, causing the door to split down the middle and light invade the darkness. Benjamin threw open the doors, tossing them on each side of the hole in the ground and proceeded up the steps.

"You still don't get it, do you?" Benjamin asked as he reached down to help Lao and Smyrna up onto grassy ground.

They both shook their heads. "So what? We all have angels that follow us," Lao said.

"Yeah," Benjamin said sickly. "But seven of those people didn't have their angels following and terrorizing them yesterday, and now they do." Benjamin looked up at the sunny sky, spreading his arms as if trying to feel the sun's rays. "Hell, some people probably haven't had their angels following them for years."

Lao and Smyrna looked at one another, as if asking the other if they understood the concern.

"Think!" he yelled. "If you are starving, you will devour anything that stands in front of you. And their angels are starving. They have been holding me for weeks trying to get a taste of my soul. But since I didn't have one, they just kept squeezing to get it out."

Lao and Smyrna started to see the bleak future as they turned toward one another.

"Yeah! Good job for figuring it out!" Benjamin said sarcastically. "If you thought the group didn't like you before, Lao..." Benjamin stopped and shook his head. "They are going to make your life a living hell. Because basically, you just let all hell break loose."

Benjamin ran away from the house down the gravel path followed by the other two.

"Why are you running?" Smyrna asked, trying to catch up.

"If you have any loved ones left, you may want to figure out how to keep them safe," he yelled. "You can try, but it's going to be much harder now."

Those words cut Lao to his heart as he looked over at Smyrna. Her eyes told Lao that she was worried too.

"Thya!"

CHAPTER 93

"What are we going to do? What are we going to do?" Smyrna repeated as her voice plummeted in fear.

Lao felt the plunge in his own chest. "I, uh, I don't know," he said stumbling over his words.

"Do they know about Thya?" Smyrna asked in dread. "Do any of those bad guys know about Thya?"

That question paralyzed Lao. He wanted to tell her that everything would be okay. He wanted to lie and convince himself that Thya was going to be safe. He wanted to look her in the eyes and tell her that no one knew about their friend.

But knowing Elijah and his crew, they probably knew all of Lao's and Smyrna's loved ones by heart.

"We have to tell her. We have to tell her to kill herself to save her," Smyrna rambled as they ran to their vehicles. "It's the only way to save her." Her words trailed like a winding path into the woods on their right.

Lao looked over into the woods and imagined a million plausible scenarios, each one ending badly. The only one that brought an ounce of relief was the thought of not losing Thya.

The only way to keep Thya safe is to kill her.

"So, how can we do this?" Lao asked as his pace quickened. "They said that we can't tell someone. That we can't warn them."

"What if they were lying? It seems like they lie about everything if it keeps them safe." They reached the country road and started toward their vehicles. "Have you ever tried telling someone?"

Lao nodded his head as he thought about Phil. "But Phil was going to be killed anyway. It might not have been my word that did it. It might have been the fact that the angel wanted to kill him."

"We have to try! Call her!"

"And say what?" Lao asked. "I'm dead, but I'm not and I'm afraid an angel of death is going to come after you?"

"I'll be here too. I'll talk to her."

Lao looked into Smyrna's eyes defeated, like a crazed man hanging onto his last thread of sanity.

"What if she doesn't want to spend eternity with us?" he asked. "Would you choose to do this?"

Lao saw the life fade from Smyrna's eyes. He knew she didn't want to live for an eternity without Phil, she had already said that. Most people are fearful of death and look at immortality as a gift, but for those that have this supposed gift, it sometimes feels like an unwanted curse.

"I don't want to lose another friend," Smyrna said with a tremble in her voice. "I don't want to watch my loved ones die with my own two eyes like you have."

They ran further up the road mulling over the idea. Lao mentally weighed the pros and cons, and even though he didn't want to lose Thya, he didn't know if he wanted her to suffer like he had been.

"I don't know about this," Lao said solemnly as they ran up to their parked vehicles.

"You've got to be kidding me," Smyrna yelled as she ran around her vehicle.

Lao looked down and saw the reason for her rage. Eight flat tires.

"They wanted to get a jump on us. They're going after our families!" Smyrna shouted as anger and fear collided. She looked at Lao as he too felt the double-sided punch. "They're going after Thya!"

CHAPTER 94

"Thya, where are you?" Lao asked with urgency as he and Smyrna were walking away from their slashed vehicle down the empty country road.

"I was in bed," Thya yawned. "It's early and a Sunday. Why are you calling?"

"I have something…" Lao started as Smyrna spoke up. "I mean, *we* have something to tell you."

"Is Smyrna with you?" Thya asked, growing alert.

"Yeah, it's me," Smyrna said as she walked beside Lao, looking up and down the road for any passing cars. "Listen to us, Thya."

"Wait, why are you two together?"

"Just listen to us," Lao said urgently.

"Okay," Thya said uncertainly.

Lao took a deep breath to gain some courage as Smyrna grabbed his hand for some emotional and physical support. "This is going to sound crazy, but you have to hear us out, okay?"

"Okay," Thya said unsure.

"Thya, Smyrna and I…well…" he stopped and looked at his friend who nodded her head.

"Well, what?" Thya asked in the silence.

"Well…we are…" he started once again.

"Thya," Smyrna said calmly. "We're immortals."

"You're what?"

"It's true, Thya," Lao reassured. "We are immortals." The two continued to walk along the uninviting road, waiting for their friend to say something. "Thya," he said gently and cautiously, "are you still there?"

"Yeah," she said with a chuckle in her voice. "What are you two on?"

237

"Nothing," Smyrna answered in haste. "We aren't on anything. It's true, Thya. It's true."

"Do you know how crazy you two sound right now?" Thya laughed out loud. "Why did you decide to try to trick me now? It's not April Fool's Day."

"It's not a trick," Lao said courageously. "It's the truth. We died, but we didn't leave."

"Wait!" Thya interrupted. "I thought you said you were immortals. Now you are saying you died? Immortals can't die."

"It's confusing, I know," Smyrna said grabbing the phone from Lao's hand. "There's a strange loophole where if you die when no one is around to see it, you become an immortal."

The two listened to Thya breathe but not say a word.

"It's true. I died on Halloween night, and then strange things started happening," Lao said as the two leaned their heads together to hear and speak into the phone. "Think about it. You thought I was acting strange right after Halloween. When Reid died. Phil. The person in the park. The waitress. Phil's mom. You saw how I reacted."

"Yeah, but that doesn't prove you're an immortal," Thya retorted. "That proves nothing."

"It proves that people die around us," Smyrna said.

"Why do people die around immortals?"

"Since we tricked death, the angel of death is acting out some type of revenge on the people around us," Smyrna answered. "It's true, Thya. When an angel picks someone to die, we can't move or do anything. We just have to freeze and watch."

"That is sick," Thya said with judgment.

"It's not our fault," Smyrna replied. "Please believe us, Thya." Her tears flowed as she reached out clutching onto Lao's hand. "Please. Please believe us."

Thya didn't respond. Lao and Smyrna continued to walk until they spotted a lone car heading their direction.

"Please, Thya," Lao said, breaking the silence. "We're trying to help you."

"Help me?" Thya scoffed. "How is telling me you have to watch people die going to help me?"

"Because if you stay in our lives," Smyrna said, stopping and looking at Lao, "alive, then eventually, you will die."

"Smyrna, that's not cool," Thya said, hanging up the phone.

"Thya?" Lao and Smyrna started saying over and over. "Thya!"

"Call again!"

Lao called Thya again, but it went straight to her voicemail. He kept calling her over and over, hoping she would eventually pick up.

As he called her for the sixth time, a car stopped, and the driver rolled down his window.

"Do you need a lift?" he asked. "I'm heading into town."

Smyrna and Lao both nodded their heads and got into the backseat.

"Were those your two cars I passed back there?" he asked, looking in the rearview mirror.

"Yeah," Smyrna said as Lao continued to redial Thya. "It looks like someone slashed our tires."

"Kids," the driver said rolling his eyes. "They think it's always about them."

"She's still not picking up," Lao said.

Smyrna patted Lao on his knee, "It's okay, Lao. We can try again later."

"So, where are you two heading?" the driver asked, unaware of the angel of death in the passenger seat.

Lao grabbed for his seatbelt trying to get Smyrna's attention as he buckled in.

Smyrna noticed the look in Lao's eyes as he sat frozen unable to move. She went for her seatbelt and tried to fit the buckle into the latch, but she was a second too late.

CHAPTER 95

"Smyrna!" Lao dangled sideways in the backseat of the twisted car as the sound of falling glass filled the void like a soothing wind chime.

"Smyrna!" Lao continued as he looked at the driver's seat in front of him. The man looked lifeless as his body hung from within the constraints of his safety belt. His bare arms, bloody and cut, dangled into the passenger seat. The angel had already taken his soul.

Lao unbuckled his seatbelt and fell to the ground, landing on the concrete through the broken window. He looked up and found an opening as the sunlight streamed in showing all the surrounding destruction. The radio continued to play as the morning disc jockey told of a glorious Sunday morning.

Lao reached up and gripped his doorframe. He pulled himself up and escaped through the broken window. He couldn't feel pain, but knew his palms would be shredded from the glass fragments. No blood was flowing, but he could see the inside of his wound.

He jumped down and shouted for Smyrna once again. He knew the driver was dead, but Smyrna had to be somewhere close by. She might have gone through the window, but she wasn't lying dead in the grass.

He was about to scream out her name once again, when he felt a punch to his gut as he thought about Branch. Branch didn't die, but the effects of the wreck remained with him. His twisted legs, his crushed face, his twisted mouth. His devastated body.

Would Smyrna's? he wondered.

He wanted to run to her rescue, but he also wanted to run away and forget about her. If she needed rescuing that meant she would need help the rest of her existence.

All because he didn't remind her to put her seatbelt on before he froze.

"Smyrna," he feebly said as he looked around the crash. He didn't shout her name. He had shouted it enough. "Smyrna," he said once again as he saw some movement in the blades of grass.

He hoped it was the wind or even a cricket causing the stirring of the ground, but hopes were dashed when he walked up.

"Smyrna!" He froze at the sight.

"Lao," she said, but he heard nothing. His hearing vanished at the sight of what used to be Smyrna. Her body looked intact with her arms and legs spread over the grass as if looking overhead and watching the clouds float by.

"Why can't I move?" Smyrna asked as Lao stooped down and brushed her hair out of her eyes.

He lifted her up and showed her.

He held her head with his hands as she looked down at her detached body still lying in the grass.

CHAPTER 96

Smyrna shrieked in horror.

"Lao! Why?" The vibrations of her scream tickled Lao's hands as he held onto the remains of his dear friend.

"Oh, Smyrna!" he moaned. "You can't die!"

"So, I'm stuck like this?" She started to hyperventilate as her eyes darted in random directions. "I'm stuck like this forever? Just a decapitated head?"

Lao went into solution mode. "We can fix this," he said raising her head so his eyes were looking into hers. "There has to be a way. We can fix this."

"How?" she cried. "How can anyone fix this?"

"There's got to be someone," he said optimistically. "There has to be someone in our condition. A scientist. A doctor. An immortal who has solved things like this."

"You really think so?"

Lao wanted to tell her the truth, but he lied instead. "Yeah, Smyrna. Someone can help us with this."

"Okay," she said weakly. "Just promise me you'll never leave me."

"I promise," he said timidly as he thought about the weight of an eternity's baggage for someone he'd just started calling a friend a month ago. "We have to leave." He looked up at the wreckage of the flipped car as a trail of smoke rose to the sky. "Someone is going to find this soon, and we need to be gone."

"We can't just leave my body," she said with a tremble in her voice as he walked away. "That's my body!"

"We have to," he said sadly. "We don't have time. We have to leave," he ran with remorse back to the car. He laid her head down beside the car and jumped into the backseat.

"Lao! Don't leave me!"

He returned after twenty seconds and stuffed her head into her purse.

"If I'm going to be like this forever, I need Thya!" she yelled as a pack of gum smacked her face when Lao started running.

He pulled out his phone and dialed again. He waited for Thya to answer, but it went to voicemail again.

"Thya! You have to believe me. Trust me! You have to trust me! Please come to the address I'm about to send to you. Come and see for yourself. I cannot force you to do anything, but if you don't want to die, please come. And be safe. Bad things are happening. People are dying. Please, be safe, Thya. Smyrna and I will be there."

He stopped talking and thought for a second as he turned off the state route, heading toward the city.

"I love you, Thya, and I don't want to live without you," he said emotionally. "I can't live without you, but if you stay alive, I'm going to have to. Because you will eventually die and I never will."

He ended the call and sent her the address of where to meet.

"How'd I do?" he asked as he continued to run at a sprinter's pace.

"I think you did good." Smyrna voice jostled from inside the purse on Lao's shoulder as her head swayed with his running motion.

He hoped he was making a good decision.

CHAPTER 97

Lao ran up the driveway past Branch's truck parked in front of the damaged garage where Phil died. He had never told either of his friends where he was living. He would make excuses any time Thya or Smyrna mentioned coming over. It was easy making up stories about his make-believe uncle. They knew nothing about Lao's uncle except he was a strict man who didn't allow friends over.

He walked into the empty house and laid Smyrna's purse on the bar counter.

"Are you okay?" He unzipped the purse and gently picked her up, brushing her hair out of her face.

"I'm okay," she said blinking her eyes. "Luckily, I don't get motion sickness anymore."

Lao smiled at her sense of humor at a horrible time.

He put her down and noticed that she wasn't level. Her head couldn't balance on its own. He needed something she could rest in.

He picked her up and started walking around the house.

"Your uncle!" she gasped.

Lao almost laughed but quickly hid his emotion. "He's out of town on business. He left this morning and won't be back for a couple of weeks."

"What are we going to do when he returns?" she asked, realizing her life would not be easy to explain.

"Don't worry about that now. We have other matters to deal with." He stopped and lifted her head so they could once again be eye to eye. "It's going to be okay. I promise."

She smiled at his optimistic leadership.

"Thank you, Lao," she said warmly. "Thank you for not leaving me."

"I wouldn't leave you." His words tasted sour, even though he couldn't taste anything. It was his guilt for thinking that same thought when he was searching the grass for her body.

"I know. You're a good guy, Lao."

He smiled at her kind words as he walked into a side bedroom. He looked around for a pedestal type stand, but found nothing.

He was about to close the door when something caught his eye.

"You'll be my bouquet every day," he smiled as he saw a clay pot with some plastic flowers on the nightstand beside the bed.

CHAPTER 98

"How is that?" Lao asked as he filled half of a clay flowerpot with marbles and buried her neck into the round glass balls. He sat her down on the bar counter that separated the kitchen from the living room and stepped away as her eyes moved around the room.

"Pretty good." She looked around the room with its furniture and pictures as if silently praising or critiquing. "This is a nice place."

"Yeah," he nodded as he looked around admiring the furnishings and décor. "It is pretty nice."

Lao's phone rang. He looked down and picked it up with trembling hands. "Thya!"

"What is going on?" she asked. Her voice sounded like tears were streaming down her cheeks.

"What do you mean?" Lao asked.

"My neighbor," she said with a jittering voice. "Her husband had a tragic accident a little while ago. My dad said he was washing his car when he drowned."

Lao looked over at Smyrna and their eyes connected.

"How do you freakin' drown while you are washing your car on a Sunday morning? How?" Thya stammered as she spoke.

"Thya, slow down," Lao said soothingly. "Breathe."

"Breathe?" Thya erupted. "Breathe is all you can say? You call me this morning and say bad things are going to be happening and now my neighbor dies tragically and all you tell me is to breathe?"

"We told you this was going to happen," Lao said gently. "I am so sorry, Thya. I know this doesn't make any sense, but you need to get over here as soon as possible."

"I'm scared. Can you please come get me?"

"No," Lao said sadly. "If I come, that could kill you."

"What about Smyrna?" She changed the call to a video call clutching her pillow under her chin like a security blanket or bullet proof vest.

"I'm sorry, but Smyrna can't come either," Lao said as Smyrna agreed in the background.

"Smyrna, please! I'm scared."

Lao didn't turn the phone around when Smyrna spoke, but kept the video on his face.

"Thya, I wish I could come and get you, but Lao is right. If we come and get you, you may die in the process."

"But I don't want to die!" she moaned as her bloodshot eyes dribbled tears. "I don't want to leave you two."

"Are you sure about that?" Lao asked.

"Yes! I don't want to die!"

"I don't want you to die either," Lao said looking away from the camera and toward Smyrna.

"Me either," Smyrna said.

"Let me see her." Thya wiped her eyes at the sound of Smyrna's comforting voice. "Let me see Smyrna."

"I don't think that's a good idea," Lao said. "You need to come over here first. That may be better."

"Lao! I'm losing it here, and I need to see my best friend. I've called her five times and she hasn't answered."

"I don't want to shock you," Smyrna said as she looked up at Lao who still had the phone recording his face.

"You won't shock me," Thya said through a whining tone. "What could shock me?"

"I've been in an accident," Smyrna said fragilely.

"Accident?" Thya squalled. "I thought you were an immortal."

"Immortals can get damaged, but we can't die," Lao said forcefully.

"Let me see her, or I'm not coming over." Thya sat on her bed and looked into the camera as her eyes darted from side to side. Her voice trembled as she pleaded. "Please, Smyrna."

Lao looked at Smyrna who nodded her head to turn the camera around. Lao zoomed in on Smyrna's face.

"You look fine to me. What are you not telling me?"

"Show her," Smyrna commanded.

Lao panned out on the camera image as Thya billowed in pain and fear.

"Oh, Smyrna!"

It was a shrill as painful as the whistler's sound to Lao's ears.

CHAPTER 99

Lao and Smyrna tried their best to explain and answer all of Thya's questions, but they still didn't know all the answers. All they knew was they didn't want to be separated from their friend, and Thya didn't want to be separated from them.

"Are you sure you want to do this?" Lao asked as he showed Smyrna's head in the flowerpot. "We can't guarantee anything."

"Oh, Lao," she swooned. "I'll happily spend forever with you two as anything, as long as we are together."

"Then come, quick!" Lao said as he looked into the camera. "And be safe. Do not go near anyone. If you see someone, stop and hide. You cannot be killed if you are not seen."

"Okay," Thya said timidly. "I'm heading your way."

"Please, Thya," Smyrna urged. "Be smart and watch your back."

Thya nodded her head and ended the call.

Lao and Smyrna looked at one another.

"What now?" Smyrna asked.

Lao shrugged his shoulders without confidence. He knew they needed to get ready for Thya. They needed to have everything ready for when she walked into the room. He knew they couldn't be around, and that thought sickened him.

Thya's biggest fear was dying alone. But in order to save her, she had to face her biggest fear.

She was going to have to die by herself.

Smyrna suddenly had an epiphany. "Do you have any pills in this house? We can leave her a note to lock the door behind her and swallow all the pills. And lock us in the bedroom."

"But what if someone looks through the window?"

"Well, then you are going to have to cover them. Look through the cabinets. Find some newspaper and cover and tape all the

250

windows. We have to make sure no one can see her die," she said urgently. "We have to make sure we don't get Thya killed."

CHAPTER 100

"Are you sure it's good enough?" Smyrna asked, eyeing the windows from the counter.

"I think so." But Lao wasn't convinced with the history he had with his nemesis. "But I've seen the angel do things."

"Do you think the angel will tear the paper?"

"I just don't feel like this is enough." Lao took a step back and stood in the middle of the darkened living room. He circled in place and hoped something would jump out at him like a warning sign.

Smyrna eyed some of the furniture and had a plan.

"Move the couch to the back door. Make sure no one can enter through it. Not even break it down and get in."

Lao quickly dragged the three-seat leather couch across the floor and put it front of the door.

"Good," Smyrna approved. "Now move the kitchen table. The more weight the better."

Lao ran like a crazy man moving the furniture around, trying to devise a fool-proof plan.

"Get a hammer and some nails," Smyrna commanded. "We have to tell her to hammer the door shut once she gets in. We can't take any chances."

Lao dashed back to the utility room and went through the cabinets. He found what he was looking for and even something better. He laid the hammer and a box of nails on the counter.

The two looked around the room.

"Is it good enough?"

"I hope it is," Smyrna said feebly. "I hope it is."

Lao walked around the windows and made sure there were no rips or tears in the three layers of coverings.

"How many pills is it going to take?" Smyrna asked as she looked over at the prescription bottles. "What if it doesn't kill her? What if it doesn't work?"

Lao reached into his pocket and pulled out a bottle that he found in the cabinet.

"If the pills don't work, this will," he said setting down the small jar with a handwritten label on it.

"What is it?"

He grabbed a cup from the cupboard and filled it halfway with water. He poured the jar's contents into the water and stirred, throwing the spoon away as the powder dissolved.

"Ricin."

CHAPTER 101

"When do you think she's going to show up?" Smyrna asked as she looked on from the nightstand.

"I don't know." Lao reclined on the bed and stared up at the ceiling, even though technically this was his bedroom, he had never spent much time in it. "I just hope she gets here safely."

The two waited in silence for the front door to open. They waited for Thya to follow the instructions Lao texted.

Suddenly, Smyrna's eyes perked up.

"Do you hear that?" she asked softly.

"No," Lao whispered, rising on his elbows to hear.

The two waited for a minute before they heard pounding.

"She's here." Smyrna smiled with her eyebrows raised in eagerness. "She's nailing the door shut."

Lao nodded his head. He heard the agonizing slamming of the hammer hitting the nails. Thya hammered for about two minutes followed by silence.

"She must be reading the letter," Smyrna said.

Lao closed his eyes and hoped their plan worked. He could picture Thya picking up the letter beside the glass of water and a bottle of prescriptions and reading it.

Thya,

I wish we could be out there with you, but we are not allowed. If we go out there, the angel of death will freeze us and force us to watch you die. But please do not fear. You may feel a little pain, but you will suddenly rise with no damage. All I have is a cut on my head from where I fell. Smyrna just had a rope mark around her neck from where she hung herself. Please take these pills and drink all the water. Then go over to the couch and lie down. Close your eyes and wait. Then when all the pain is gone, you will feel no pain ever again. And we will never be apart. Forever. I love you, Thya. I know Smyrna loves you as well. We are just in the other room. We are here with you. You are not dying alone. We are here.

Lao

Lao could visualize Thya holding the cup of water and looking at the white pills. He wanted nothing more than to ease her fear.

"Do you think she has done it yet?" Smyrna whispered, looking tenderly at Lao.

"I don't know."

"How will we know when it's safe to come out?"

As Smyrna said those last words, they heard Thya scream.

"Oh, Thya," Smyrna moaned in pain for the girl who was more like a sister than a friend. "Should the pills put her in this much pain?"

Lao was about to answer when he heard Thya scream out again.

"Who are you!"

"What? Don't you ramemer me?"

Lao's eyes widened in horror at the voice.

"Branch!"

CHAPTER 102

"Lao!" Smyrna screamed as Lao jumped up from the bed and ran to the door. "If you go out there, the angel is going to force you to watch her die!"

"Lao!" Thya screamed at the top of her lungs. "Smyrna! Help me! There's a monster out here!"

"Thya!" Lao shouted from the door, holding the doorknob in his hand. "We've killed her!" he said to Smyrna on the nightstand. "We've just killed our friend!"

"Please! Help me!" Thya screamed through the door. "Stay back! Just stay away!" she screamed through horrific tears.

"Smyrna!" Lao leaned his back against the door and looked at Smyrna in the flowerpot seeing how quickly things can mess up. "What have we done?" He replayed the frantic morning and wondered how they had gotten here.

"You can go out there!" Smyrna said frantically. "You just can't see her."

"How can I do that?" Lao shouted as Thya continued to scream for help behind the door. "How can I go out there without seeing her?"

Smyrna's eyes moved over to a dresser with a mirror over it. Her eyes fixed on something on its surface.

"What?" Lao looked to the dresser. Suddenly, he saw the answer to his hopes.

He ran over and grabbed the pair of scissors and plunged the blade into his right eye. He didn't feel a thing, just blackness. He gripped the handle and repeated the process. His left eye went dark.

"Now go! Save our girl!"

"Thya!" Lao ran out of the bedroom, feeling for the hallway's walls, but he felt more hinderance than helpful.

"Lao! Help me!" she screamed in the distance.

Lao felt along the wall until he came into the living room.

"Where's Branch?" Lao was blind by his own choosing, but his hearing hadn't caught up to its dominate sense. "You have to warn me where Branch is!"

"He's crawling on the ground!" she shouted up ahead through her sobs. "Lao!"

"Where?"

"Ello Lao," Branch said as if wanting to play a game of Marco Polo.

"He's heading your way! Watch out!"

Lao bent his legs, reaching toward the ground, feeling for the intruder heading his way.

"He's on your left, Lao!" she screamed as her fear increased her volume and tears. "What happened to him? Why is this happening?"

"He ushed me down da cella!" Branch groaned as he crawled slowly, moving only one arm.

"You pushed him down the cellar?" Thya sickly moaned. "You pushed him down the cellar?" Thya's moans turned to outrage. She screamed without saying a word. Her gut churned in the horror of what she was seeing. A crippled man crawling toward her blind boyfriend.

"Where is he?" Lao's arms hung low, swaying back and forth reaching for Branch's body, but he still hadn't felt him. "Branch! Where are you!" Lao swung his arms like punches and hook shots when he heard it. He looked up instinctively. He hoped it was Branch bumping his body into the floor, but he was fearful it was someone he loved instead.

He heard a loud thump.

257

CHAPTER 103

"Thya!" Lao shouted. "Thya!"

"She gone," Branch laughed hysterically.

"No!" Lao moaned as he jumped forward, hurling his body toward the ground.

He found Branch, and the two rolled around on the floor. Lao still had two good legs and arms. He punched Branch in what he thought was his face, hitting him a few times and missing and hitting the floor a couple of times.

Branch froze. He stopped speaking. He stopped moving. He stopped everything.

Lao knew why.

Lao reached up feeling around at Branch's face to cover his eyes, but his head kept moving, breaking away from his grasp.

"Stop! Stop killing!"

Lao tried to dig his fingers into Branch's eyes, but there was some sort of protection. He couldn't dig into the skin. He couldn't blind him.

"Please!"

No matter how much Lao pleaded, he knew it wouldn't do any good. He had to get him to face away from Thya.

He stood up and grabbed Branch's legs by the ankles and pulled back. But he was barely moving him.

"Come on!" Lao groaned in agony, trying to keep his footing on the living room floor. He pulled again with all of his strength feeling Branch move slightly.

That little inch gave Lao the hope he needed.

He tugged harder than he had ever before. He dug into Branch's muddy jeans, knowing in his heart that Thya was going to be saved. He jolted his body one last time and felt the world slide with him.

But instead of Branch moving, it was just his torn, tattered jeans.

Lao fell back. He tried to keep his balance and get his footing back. He tried to catch himself on the floor to start again.

But he didn't feel a crash.

He was falling.

And falling.

And falling.

CHAPTER 104

"No!" Lao fell back, hurdling into the darkness. He thought the fall was going to be forever, but it eventually stopped.

He hit the ground.

He felt his hands along the ground, but it didn't feel like the living room hardwood floor. It was grimy and slippery.

He tried to stand up, but his legs couldn't move. He felt down his torso and found his legs twisted and broken in different directions.

"Thya!" Lao's yell echoed around him, making him feel like there were a hundred Laos screaming below.

"She's ot ead et!" Branch screamed from above. "Ut she oon ill be!"

"No!" Lao translated those frightening words. *She's not dead yet. But she soon will be!*

Lao looked up into the darkness. He couldn't see anything but a little light overhead. He couldn't see the image of Branch looking down into the cellar from the safety of the living room floor. He couldn't see the depth of the well to calculate how much he would have to climb. He couldn't see that the climb would be impossible with his disfigured limbs.

"Thya!"

"Ot et," Branch softly soothed.

Not yet.

"Please! No!" Lao pleaded. "Not for me, but for Thya!"

He thought he heard Smyrna's faint voice from inside the house calling for Thya.

"Smyrna! I'm so sorry! Thya! I'm sorry!" Lao moaned in pain as he knew the horrific news that would soon be uttered. He knew, and that caused even more pain, knowing the inevitable was happening and he couldn't do anything but lie and wait.

Branch leaned over the end of the hole.

"Se's ed," he sinisterly laughed. "Se's ed! Se's ed! Se's ed!"

She's dead!

"No!" Lao screamed as the words echoed down the well.

"I, Ao," he hissed as the light overhead vanished when the door shut overhead.

Those words caused a chill to run through Lao's body. Those words were going to haunt him until someone could rescue him. Those words were not worth the scissors in the end.

Bye, Lao.

CHAPTER 105

Lao lay in the same spot. He wondered how long he had been in the cellar, and it sickened him to wonder how long he would have to lie there. How many days had passed? Or how many years had passed? Or generations? He couldn't tell night from day. He couldn't hear Branch overhead, but he knew nothing other than he was down in the cellar and no one knew.

No one except Branch, and he wasn't telling anyone.

Guilt weighed heavily on Lao as he replayed the last moments over and over. He wondered what would have happened if he had gone right instead of left. Or, if he had given Thya a less deadly dose, would he have been able to move Branch so he couldn't watch Thya die? What if he'd never moved the couch away from the cellar door? It seemed like remorse filled his insides like blood used to fill his veins.

As if the guilt over Thya wasn't enough, he dreaded to consider what was happening to Smyrna. He could still hear her request for Lao to take care of her. And he could still hear himself promise her he would.

He wondered if Smyrna was still sitting in the flowerpot in the bedroom. At least she had some light. Or maybe Branch had found her and was torturing her too.

That thought sickened him.

He had let down his two closest friends in a matter of minutes. Everything fell apart in a stab of two eyes.

It seemed like whenever Lao would stop thinking of Smyrna he would cycle back and dwell on his suffering.

Then he would dwell on Thya.

Then he would dwell on Smyrna.

And then repeat once again.

It was a cycle he wanted to end.

He hoped for the day that a new owner would buy the house and rescue him, but would Branch ever sell his house? He was an immortal too. He could be the owner of the house forever.

That thought frightened Lao.

He could be stuck down in the well forever with no hope of ever getting out.

But suddenly something new rattled his senses. He looked up but saw nothing new. Just blackness.

He swore he'd heard something different.

CHAPTER 106

Lao's ears sharpened. He thought he heard something that sounded like breathing. Or maybe it was just his hopeful thinking.

He waited for what seemed like hours, or even days, for the sounds to clarify.

And eventually they did. It was whistling.

His body tightened as the whistling started to echo. Lao lay there unmovable until he heard another whistling.

He hoped the angels had found some mercy, and a rescue was within reach. He hoped, but he knew such optimism could be dangerous.

The whistling suddenly stopped, replaced by words. He was hearing a conversation.

"Some never come to terms with the fact that everything they see is not as it seems."

"Yeah, but I messed up in places. When I got the sundae, I thought I blew my cover for sure, Max. I didn't know Thya didn't like nuts or cherries. Or when I messed up on the place of the first date. That wasn't in the character portrayal I was given."

"Even the best writers miss things here and there, Jade," Max consoled.

"Well, the mother even said his name wrong once," Jade commented.

"Yeah, but they weren't that close. He probably didn't realize it was a mistake. But they rarely see it because it doesn't seem believable."

"Believable," they laughed. "Who would believe this? But they always do," Jade answered. "You did a good job playing, Phil. You've really improved from the first role you played."

"Thanks, I guess talent takes time. But to be honest, I thought the script was farfetched with telling him he was an immortal that died in the graveyard, but he seemed to believe it," Max said.

"They believe anything they're told."

"But we still aren't allowed to tell him, right?"

"Correct. He has to figure out the truth for himself, so now we just watch and wait."

"It may take a while for him to realize he actually died when he was hit by the car that Halloween night," Max stopped. "Stupid boy, he should have looked both ways when he was crossing the road. Humans - they think they are unstoppable, but when a car hits you, that's hard to live through. And to think he was already dead in the woods walking to the cemetery and he couldn't even see it. But they eventually do. They eventually see the truth."

"That's my favorite part," Jade whispered.

"Mine too."

"I can't wait until he discovers he's not immortal and he's been in Hell this whole time and we're just pretending to be his friends and family to torment him. Makes the job worth it," Jade remarked as the two demons laughed wickedly.

Wait. What? I'm in Hell?

EPILOGUE

Laonardo "Lao" Eden died on October 31st at 6:04 p.m. when an unknown driver struck the teenager as he was crossing the road at the corner of Trimborn Avenue and Highway 427. He is survived by his parents, Rufus and Jillian Eden, and his grandmother Radi Gindle. He was an avid swimmer who always looked for the best in people.

If anyone has any information on the unknown driver, please call the authorities. Funeral arrangements will be announced soon.

THE FUNERAL

Thya sat in the back pew of the small country church dressed in a black polka dot dress waiting for her friends to join her in her time of mourning. She held her phone in her lap and reread the last texts they exchanged.

What? Do you expect the ghosts to be gone soon? Lao texted.

You think you're funny, don't you? She had replied.

A tear rolled down her cheek as she scrolled to the top of her texts, dating back before they were officially seeing one another. She had reread the thousands of texts over the last two days as if they were love letters for their tech generation.

"Thya," Smyrna said, shaking in all black as she stood beside the pew. Thya stood up and hugged her friend as they both wailed.

"I still can't believe this is happening," Smyrna said as they sat down, holding each other's hand for support.

"I can't either." Thya looked down at Smyrna's hand, seeing the ring Phil had gotten her for her last birthday. She looked at her fingers and knew she would never have such a treasured gift from her love.

"Do the cops know anything yet?"

Thya shrugged her shoulders as she looked ahead at Lao's grieving family standing beside the casket. She hadn't gotten the nerve to walk up and look at him yet. She kept imagining this was just a horrid dream. She still hoped that at any minute she would wake and Lao would send her a new text about going to the movies tonight. She looked down at her phone.

There were no new texts from Lao.

The back door of the church opened with a gust of wind, followed by a large group of students. Reid led the solemn procession of swimmers down the center aisle.

Reid waved to Thya as he walked by and then lowered his head.

"Is Phil coming?" Thya asked as she watched her friends from school stand silently in line to give their condolences.

""He should be on his way."

The two sat in silence, staring at the mahogany casket as Lao's mother hugged every swimmers neck. Thya knew she needed to stand up and see Lao one last time, but every time she tried to move in that direction, her legs wouldn't let her.

"How's his mother doing?" Smyrna asked, still clutching onto Thya's hand.

"I don't know. I haven't gone down there yet."

"You've never met, have you?"

Thya shook her head as another tear rolled down her cheek. She needed to go down and hug Lao's mother. She wanted nothing more than to tell her how much she loved him. She longed to tell all the stories they had shared in the last few months. But she couldn't. She just sat in the back pew hoping this was just a bad dream.

Smyrna looked down at her watch and then the back door. "It's about to begin, Thya. If you want to see him, you have to go now." Smyrna whispered these kind words into Thya's ear as she squeezed her hand tighter. "I'll go with you."

Thya turned her head and nodded.

They both stood up with their fingers interlocked, walking down the center aisle in unison.

"I'm sorry for your loss, Mrs. Eden," Smyrna said as she hugged the red-eyed mother.

"Thank you," she answered as she blew her nose with a floral lace handkerchief.

Thya stood there silently, looking into the casket. She stared at the shoes because they could have been anyone's feet. Then she drifted her eyes up to the khaki slacks. Her throat clenched at the sight of his belt.

She noticed it was the one she used to mock with a swimming motif sewn into the blue threads.

Her legs wobbled as she moved her eyes further up, seeing a nicely pressed gingham blue shirt he had worn to the school dance. She closed her eyes and took a breath as teardrops trickled down her numb cheeks.

She exhaled and opened her eyes, awakening herself from the delusional hope. She reached out her hand and felt his cheek. Her insides froze from the coldness of his skin. She moaned in painful cries as she pulled back her hand wishing she had never touched him.

"Lao!" she cried as Smyrna held onto her side.

"Were you and Lao close?"

Thya turned around seeing an older woman in a long black gown walking up from behind with her arms opened wide.

"We were, we were," she said, but she couldn't get the words out between her sobs.

"This is Thya, Lao's girlfriend," Smyrna kindly introduced. "And you must be his grandmother."

The older woman nodded and looked into Thya's eyes. "You're a very pretty girl. Lao was lucky to have you."

Thya shook her head and continued to cry, falling into Lao's grandmother's arms. Her arms were firm, yet gentle. She sunk deeper into Lao's grandmother's arms and released all the emotions she had been holding in for the last few days.

"Just let it out, child," she soothed as she brushed Thya's hair, rocking her in her arms. "Just let it out."

"Why did this happen?" Thya cried.

"I don't know why God allows things like this to happen," she said with strength in her words. "But the only saving grace I have is knowing Lao is in a better place."